SHANNON'S LAW

A gripping, action-packed thriller

PAUL BENNETT

Nick Shannon Thriller Book 6

Joffe Books, London
www.joffebooks.com

First published in Great Britain in 2022

This paperback edition was first published
in Great Britain in 2022

ISBN: 978-1-80405-288-4

'*Scams are tricky to pull off — they require a lot of organization and attention to detail — but then they're easy to get away with: you simply disappear. Frauds are easy to do, but it's hard to get away with. Whichever, we're coming for you.*'

CHAPTER ONE

Rarely has there been less mourning than at the death of the Home Secretary. It wasn't that he was a two-faced politician — one becomes conditioned to that — but a murderer: the hit-and-run driver who had crippled my sister and killed her innocent boyfriend. I had spent seven years in prison for the assisted suicide of Susie, sixteen years old at the time and full of life, and a further eight years tracking down the driver before finally getting the ultimate form of justice. Persistence pays.

Since the Home Secretary's death, business for Shannon Investigations had been booming, we had to reorganize the company to cope with the rise in demand. We were forensic accountants — in layman's terms, fraud detectives. My role in the Home Secretary's death said we don't take prisoners: no one is too big to escape from us, and we never give up. Good reputation to have.

I'd entered the building housing the offices of the legal firm of Ackroyds in the barrister country of Temple via an unnecessary porch which only served to house a fire alarm — a fire alarm in the area farthest away from the staff? — and an elephant's foot umbrella stand. I was sitting in the reception area mulling over life's rich pageant while awaiting my meeting with the senior partner. There was a lot of brown furniture around, some of the pieces genuine antiques by the battered look of them. The walls were an uninspiring shade of magnolia and the chair I was sat on had a straight back and would be uncomfortable if you had to spend more than a quarter of an hour in it. There were some old copies of a golf magazine to riffle through. The whole set-up needed some love and affection. The vibes were not good.

Behind a reception desk sat a woman whose badge told everyone her name was Nancy. When was the last time you met a woman called Nancy? She was so focused on her computer screen that she failed to register me when I first walked in. I could have been wearing a striped jumper and carrying a bag marked SWAG for all she knew. Not a good start: you have to keep a mental record of comings and goings as a receptionist. She was wearing glasses secured round her neck by a chain, evidently in case she forgot where she had left them. She looked close to sixty, in a twinset and simulated pearls — there were too many of them to be real, or maybe I'm just too used to seeing fakes. She was doing her best in working a switchboard while typing up a document of what I presumed was a piece of unintelligible legal jargon that deserved her full attention. Or maybe no one would notice if it was full of mistakes. I mean, who reads all that stuff anyway? Other lawyers, I guess. It's a self-perpetuating vicious circle.

'Mr Shannon, I presume?' she said.

I bet that when she used these words, a smart-ass visitor would reply, 'Well, I'm certainly not Dr Livingstone.'

'Well, I'm certainly not Dr Livingstone,' I said.

Always start as you mean to go on.

At three p.m. precisely, a woman in her sixties arrived in the reception area and asked me to follow her. She took me along a corridor and stopped outside a large oak door. I opened the door for her and followed her inside. The room was pretty much what one could expect judging from the reception area. More brown furniture, including, fittingly, a partners' desk with a dark green leather top and gold edging. Behind the desk was a set of French doors, open to provide a breath of fresh air, and leading out to a small courtyard.

A man stood up from a leather seat behind the desk. He looked to be in his seventies and was wearing a full three-piece suit in dark grey. There was a chain attached to his waistcoat and it seemed a fair bet that there was a watch leading from it.

He extended his hand and I shook it.

'Ackroyd,' he said. 'Roger Ackroyd — my parents were fans of Agatha Christie.'

'Shannon,' I said. 'Please call me Nick.'

'No, no,' he said. 'I don't think that would be appropriate, young man.'

Young man? Everything is relative, I suppose.

He motioned me to sit down while the woman, named Beryl from her tag, made her exit. On the desktop, otherwise largely unadorned, sat a cake with a knife and two small plates. Alongside were two sherry glasses which sparkled in the sun coming through the French doors. 'I like to take a little cake and a glass of Madeira at this time in the afternoon,' he said. 'Will you join me? Do say yes — I hate drinking alone.'

'It will be my pleasure,' I said. 'Been a long while since I last had a glass of Madeira.'

He walked across the office to one of the wooden filing cabinets and took a decanter from the topmost drawer. He came back and poured a measure into the two glasses on the tray. He placed one before me and took a sip from his glass.

'Civilized way to start the afternoon,' he said, sighing wistfully.

Three p.m. and it's the start of the afternoon? Maybe he had a nap after a steak and kidney pie for lunch.

'So,' I began. 'How can we help?' The Madeira was the sweet variety, like an Oloroso sherry, and went perfectly with the slice of golden syrup sponge cake, although it would mask anything less subtle. I studied him while he chewed on the

3

cake. He had a florid complexion — if he had Madeira at three p.m. each day, that was no surprise — and a broad smile which made him look like everyone's favourite uncle or grandfather who usually handed out toffees.

'I'm the senior partner,' he said. 'Son of the founder, with no one to pass it on to — neither of my sons have any interest in the law. I have fifty-one per cent of the firm and I'm being encouraged to retire.' He shrugged. 'Maybe they're right. My time has gone. I'm a dinosaur in this modern world. The problem is that none of the other partners can afford to buy me out. So, it has been decided that the best way out of this dilemma is to merge with another firm which has the cash available to acquire us — more of a takeover, if I care to admit it. The current partners can be smaller fish in a bigger pond. But for the deal to go ahead, we need someone to value each firm and decide on the apportioning of the future shareholding. That's where you come in.'

'I would have thought your accountants would do that.'

'There's the rub,' he said. 'We need someone who is impartial.'

'So you don't trust their accountants.'

'And they don't trust ours.'

'So I'm going to be piggy in the middle?'

'For which you will be paid handsomely.'

'For which I'm grateful. I'll try to be as inconspicuous as possible. A couple of questions before I start. How does the share system work, and how do they become partners?'

'Each solicitor is paid a basic salary. Then they earn partner points from a number of criteria — the amount of business handled, the profitability of that business, the value of new clients brought in and so on. When the target is met, they are invited to become a partner.'

'And does the number of points determine the share they will get when they become a partner?'

'No, that is decided by the Partners' Committee.'

'And who sits on the committee?'

'Myself and two of the other partners.'

I had an inkling of the answer to my next question, but it had to be asked. 'Is the voting of those on the committee one-man-one-vote?'

'No, the decision is taken according to shareholding.'

'So at the moment it is effectively your vote that counts, since you hold fifty-one per cent of the shares?'

He nodded.

'And so, when the next partner is appointed, if that solicitor is given more than one per cent, you lose your majority vote?'

'That is correct. Wouldn't be right to do it any other way.'

I was sure there could well be some who thought differently. Made it an even better time to sell up.

He took a sheet of paper out of his desk drawer and passed it to me.

'There are the details of the two current partners and their shareholdings, in case you want to talk to them. Anything else, just ask my secretary, Beryl — she's been with me for twenty invaluable years.'

'I certainly will. One last question for the moment. Who is responsible for the accounts function?'

'That would be Sarah Jenkins. I've forewarned her that you will be coming. I've told her that you would require access to all the accounts, just like if you were auditors, and that I suspected you would be disruptive.'

'Correct. Although I'll try to keep that to a minimum. I'll bring along my junior; she'll keep me in check.'

'Good.' He clapped his hands together. 'Another glass to seal the deal?'

Why not? Can't be anything wrong with a couple of glasses of Madeira. Sun must be over the yardarm somewhere in the world.

He poured and we clinked our glasses.

'To success,' I said.

'To success,' he echoed.

And that's how this sorry mess started.

CHAPTER TWO

I took the Docklands Light Railway to Island Gardens with its spooky foot tunnel under the Thames to Greenwich, then walked the short distance to our home and office. The building was an old warehouse of five storeys. It had been faithfully restored by Norman, my business partner, after having acquired it by nefarious means in an insurance fraud we had been investigating. Details? Don't ask! Norman was my cellmate in Chelmsford prison where I spent the bulk of my sentence. I had spent a couple of months in Brixton while on remand, and then, after sentencing, the rest of my time in the lower-category Chelmsford. Norman was the one who saved me from going completely stir crazy by persuading me to do a correspondence course in accountancy. Sounds boring, but it turned out to be the opposite.

Norman had been sentenced because of an embezzlement fraud. He had taken a million pounds from his too-trusting employer, hidden it away where no one could find it and then given himself up so that he could spend the rest of his life at leisure and wouldn't have to be peering over his shoulders all the time. Restitution was never an option in Norman's plan. The swindled firm had claimed on its insurance and everyone was happy — bar the insurance company, I presumed, but who was bothered about that? — and went on with their life as normal. No one in the police cared anymore: long forgotten over the last fifteen years. Norman bankrolled our business while I did the bulk of the donkey work. He was a shrewd friend and mentor who was always there for advice on the finer points of fraud. Whatever Norman landed in, he came up smelling of roses. Good to always have luck, or experience or whatever it was, on your side.

The bottom floor of the converted warehouse contained one large office for myself — six-foot-two, eyes of blue, as the song goes — a reception area, a smaller office for our factotum and an informal sitting room that overlooked the Thames and housed the vitally important coffee machine. The next floor up was used by us as a gathering point when work had finished for the day. The floor above that was Norman's accommodation which he shared with Morag, our receptionist and general assistant — with whom he was totally smitten — who had previously been PA to the Chief Constable of Mid Anglia Police Force. Anji, our junior member of staff, had moved into the vacant floor above that — the arrangement with her seemed to make sense given the unpredictability of our working hours and paying out rent on her small flat. It cemented her into the team, too. Anji was feisty enough to sit wherever the hell she wanted.

The topmost was my living area and bedroom. I shared that floor with Cherry Walker, what the Americans call my 'main squeeze': not exactly fitting, as that implies there was at least one other squeeze and a lot of chauvinism.

The five of us were perched on three Chesterfields arranged in an open square in the area overlooking the Thames. We were sipping some of the best coffee in London and winding down for the day. I was waiting mischievously for someone to crack, although I knew it would be Cherry. She was way back in the queue when God handed out patience.

'Well,' she said. 'Don't keep us in suspense. How did it go with Ackroyd?'

'It was interesting,' I said. 'The firm hasn't got into the twenty-first century yet — I'm not even sure it has got past the nineteenth. We had a tea ceremony at three p.m. — sponge cake and Madeira. I wouldn't be surprised if they don't keep the accounts in leather-bound ledgers written with a quill pen by a thin man sitting on a high stool. Ackroyd, though, seemed like what he would call a good egg.'

'Good to work for such people,' Norman said. 'Did you sniff anything?'

'Too early to say, but I suspect there'll be holes in their antiquated systems that a fraudster could easily slip through.'

'What's the plan?' said Anji.

'Tomorrow, Cherry and I will go to the other side of the equation — Randalls. Introduce ourselves and start the ball rolling on going through their books. After that you're on your own, Cherry, with occasional appearances by me to test the warmth of the water and the likely fit with Ackroyds. If you feel you can handle it, that is. Good to have help around when you might need it.'

'I spent more years in the Fraud Squad than I like to remember,' she replied. 'This will be a breath of fresh air. Don't worry, though. If I feel out of my depth, I won't hesitate to call for help.'

'And, Anji,' I said, 'after that, you're with me. Time for you to be blooded.'

'So,' she said 'I guess I shouldn't be wearing the thigh boots, tank top and skater skirt? Back to the black knee-length suit, white blouse and kitten heels.'

'And don't forget the glasses with the plain lenses.'

'You got it.'

'I imagine,' I continued, 'that we should be finished in a week, two at most, so, Morag, can you start making some briefing meetings with those prospective clients on the waiting list?'

'I'll start first thing,' she said in her educated Edinburgh accent that got Norman so weak at the knees.

'I'll be backstop,' he said. 'Ready to jump in if anyone needs help or a fresh approach.'

'Then only one thing left to do.'

'And what's that?' asked Anji.

'What we always do when we get a new client — open a bottle of fizz.'

* * *

'You don't need to worry, Shannon,' said Walker. We had called each other by our surnames so long that it was hard to break the habit, especially at times of stress. 'I can do it. And I won't alienate anyone. The time in the Fraud Squad is in the past — this is a new me.'

It was hard to doubt anything that she said. She was beautiful — probably the most beautiful woman I had ever come across. Her mixed-race heritage had given her a skin of coffee-and-cream colour. Her eyes were the deepest brown, verging on black; they were mesmerizing pools you could get sucked into. She was very tall and very slim, with everything in the right place. I was indeed a very lucky man.

I took her by the shoulders and drew her close to me.

'We're a new team,' I said. 'It's going to take us all a while to bed in and find our new roles. I think you'll have the hardest job of all of us. In the Fraud Squad, you were used to not being questioned. Your subordinates wouldn't dare. Even your boss deferred to you. Now it's going to be very different. Clients can be defensive and will ask you for reasons why they should listen to you. It will also seem at times that we will doubt you, when all we're trying to do is dig deep. Stick with it, Walker. You'll do fine. I promise.'

'One last question before we get into bed.'

'Yes?'

She grinned. 'Any of that champagne left?'

I laughed back. 'You're going to fit in just great.'

CHAPTER THREE

You can tell a lot about a company by its reception area. It's the outward face, the initial impression, the first telltale signs of the personality of the business. Whereas Ackroyds said *solid* and *reliable* in hushed tones, Randalls screamed *clinical, slick*. If Ackroyds was the dependable wife, Randalls was the mistress. There was a lot of chrome and smoked glass around and not much class.

Cherry and I were sitting in director's chairs waiting for our audience with the eponymous head of the practice. Randall made us wait exactly ten minutes, so that we were clear about our status.

We followed a young woman dressed in a short black dress and heels through a wide door into a large office with two solid black tables with chrome legs and half a dozen chairs set meeting-style. Randall stood up and extended his hand.

'Richard Randall,' he said, thrusting out his hand. 'Call me Dicky.'

He was tall and slim with a full head of blond hair — if it was natural — with a hint of gel to keep it under control. His blue pinstripe suit fitted him perfectly. He looked self-satisfied.

I introduced Cherry and myself, and he smiled. I almost expected to see a gold tooth glinting back at me.

'What do you think of the job?' he asked. 'Bit out of your normal line of work, eh?'

'Should be a lot easier,' I said. 'Is everybody on board?'

'Maybe not unanimous, but Ackroyd and I agree it has to be done. What did you think of him?'

'I liked him. Cherry hasn't met him yet — she'll be handling your side, while I do Ackroyds.'

'It will be a pleasure.' He just about managed to say the words without a leer. I felt sorry for Cherry. Maybe we should swap jobs.

I cleared my throat. 'We will, of course, swap over at times, so that each of us can absorb the ethos of both practices,' I said, in preparation of giving Cherry a break from his lasciviousness from time to time.

'Did Ackroyd explain the rationale?' Randall asked, finally dragging his eyes away from her.

'We're pretty clear,' I said. 'Elaborating wouldn't go amiss, though.'

'It's primarily about letting him retire without too many waves,' he continued, businesslike. 'It's a family firm, and he wants to look after his staff as if they were his progeny. The world of law has changed. It's all about big firms or an increasing number of one-man bands — there's no in-between anymore. No middle ground. We intend to be big. The call nowadays is for specialists — conveyancing, litigation, company law, family and so on. The days of the family solicitor you went to for all your needs are numbered. I can make the generalists of Ackroyds into specialists.'

'And there's a lot of synergy to go with it?' Cherry said.

Randall nodded his head. 'Much of the backroom staff can go. It's only the solicitors we're interested in. And the client list that goes with them, of course.'

'Naturally,' I said. He was going to asset-strip the place. And next year, it would be someone else, another company, until he was satisfied that Randalls could not easily get any bigger or more streamlined.

'How many partners?' I asked. 'How many to persuade to get behind the effective takeover?'

'There are twelve partners, and some of the others will agitate to become one when the situation changes with the takeover. The shares currently vary, from twenty per cent down to five.'

'With you being the twenty per cent, I presume,' said Cherry.

He nodded proudly.

'We'll need details of all staff, particularly the solicitors,' I said, 'with as much financial detail as is available — level of business handled, profit margins and so on, the last three years of accounts and any recent figures you have.'

'Okay.' He nodded. 'How long will it take you?'

'If there are no problems — which I don't anticipate at the moment, it all sounds straightforward — a week of both of our time should do it, two weeks maximum. We'll try to minimize any disruption. You'll hardly know we're here. You're happy with our terms of business — daily rate plus ten per cent of any frauds discovered?'

'Yes, though I doubt you will find anything. My PA will give you the signed contract and arrange for anything you need. When can you start?'

'No time like the present,' I said. 'Who's the next biggest shareholder after yourself?' I said.

'That would be Honeywell.'

'Then we'll see him now. Have you got a room we can use?'

'Again, my PA will sort you out one.'

He stood up and gave another of his smiles, directed more at Cherry than me, and ushered us out the door. Audience over. On with business. Back to making money.

* * *

Randall's PA was a well-built woman around thirty in a short dark-blue dress, a light-blue tight-fitting top and a pair of strappy sandals with heels that must have been killing her feet by the end of the day. Her name was Jane, and she efficiently gave us copies of the accounts and the last month's update to cover the current position. *Keep on top of things* is the mantra — don't wait till the end of the year before the figures tell you that the firm's in trouble. We left our things in a small office before following her to Honeywell.

Honeywell was a tall, gaunt man in his forties. His face was thin and pockmarked from adolescent acne and he wore a light grey suit with a pink shirt and a dark-blue tie. If he'd taken his jacket off, I would have bet good money that he'd be wearing a pair of braces. Overall, he gave the impression that he was in the wrong job: trader on the floor of the Stock Exchange seemed more his style.

His office was a large room reflecting his position in the pecking order. There was a big wide print of sketches of animals by Picasso in a black frame. It introduced a rakish element to the plain apple-white walls. His desk was covered in plastic files labelled with yellow Post-it notes and containing impressively thick piles of paper.

We introduced ourselves and sat down before he could tell us he was too busy to talk. Instead, he shook our hands and frowned.

'How long will this take?' he said.

'About an hour at the most,' I said.

He gulped.

'Tell us a little about yourself?' Cherry asked brightly, ignoring his obvious reluctance. 'Your background and what you do here.'

'Nigel Honeywell. Forty years old. Married with two children. Law degree from Sussex. Been here ten years. Poached from a firm not too far from here. Handy for my commute from Highgate. It was hard to resist what Randall offered me — despite his faults, Dicky pays well. I'm a corporate lawyer with some big names on my client list — blue chip, some of them. Mergers, acquisition, employment law, defence against cases that some disgruntled employee wanted to take to a tribunal. Good reputation among my clients. My life in a nutshell.'

As he spoke, he gave off a lot of nervous energy — he kept raking his hair, cleaning his black-framed round glasses, waving his hands. I wondered whether he was always like this, or if it was our role and presence that was causing all the displacement activity.

'You said "despite his faults" about Mr Randall,' I said. 'Without wishing to tell tales out of school, can you elaborate?'

'He wants to be the biggest there is or as close to it as possible. Won't be long after the Ackroyd takeover when he gobbles up someone else. He values growth highly. As I said, he pays well, but demands a lot in return. No one here goes home at five thirty. Unpaid overtime is at least an hour, maybe two, a day. It's a sweatshop.'

'What about profitability?' Cherry asked. 'If it's growth against profitability, what side does he favour?'

'Both,' Honeywell said. 'Everyone is set targets on the volume of work and the profit margin it produces. As I said, it's a sweatshop.'

'How do you feel about the Ackroyds' deal?' I said. 'For or against?'

'They won't know what's hit them,' he said, shaking his head. 'Poor souls. They will have to fit in with us rather than vice versa. Gone will be the cosy family feel. It will all be about business from now on.'

'And how will it affect you personally?' Cherry asked.

'Depends what value you put on each practice. Profits will go up, so there'll be a bigger pool of money shared among the partners. The big question is how much my shareholding will be diluted. Does my money go up or down?'

'If you were in Roger Ackroyd's shoes, what would you do?' asked Cherry.

He gave a humourless smile. 'Run a mile,' he said. 'Within six months, you won't know Ackroyds ever existed.

If you value freedom, stay where you are. Retire and pass the reins to someone else. Recruit a new leader to take control if the current partners aren't capable of doing the job. Save the good parts, but move into modern times.'

'Would you be up for the job?' I asked. 'Were you approached about it?'

'Interesting question,' he said. 'I've thought about it a lot recently. Ackroyd did approach me a few weeks ago. I think he was exploring all options. Apparently he asked around for a new senior partner and my name came up — he obviously didn't have much faith in his two existing partners. I think I would be up for it, on the right terms. The money would have to be right. The shareholding, too. Ackroyd could retain his shares for a while. There's two partners with ten per cent each. He would have to give me the twenty-nine per cent of unissued shares with an option to buy more shares over time.'

'So, what did you say to him about the proposal?' Cherry asked.

'That I'd need to think about it. It would be a challenge, certainly, it would be like they say of football managers: can they win over the dressing room? I'd have to make redundancies. Given that, could I win over the remaining staff and get their loyalty? Time will tell. And your valuation is another factor. Could it influence the decision? Whatever happens, could you call the shots? Make the right path clear?' He smiled again. 'I think I'll stay on the right side of you. It all seems pretty moot now, though. Your presence suggests the takeover is a done deal.'

'Whatever we recommend, it will be done with complete impartiality,' I said.

He nodded. 'Okay. But right now,' he said, 'I'd like to get on with work or I won't be leaving till eight p.m. at the earliest.'

'Ever hear the phrase, "feel like a cog in something turning"?' I asked him.

'All the time,' he replied.

* * *

Cherry and I walked along the Strand and went into a coffee shop. We sat at a window looking out at pedestrians hurrying along the busy street. I stirred sugar into my double espresso and looked across the table at Cherry.

'What do you think of Randall?' I asked.

'I don't trust him an inch. He'll hoover up the Ackroyd business and pick the bones clean, if you don't mind the mixed metaphors. It's going to be a big culture shock for the remaining employees. It'll become a factory, a sweatshop, like Honeywell said. Does Ackroyd really know what he's doing?'

I nodded in agreement. 'Any other general observations before we get to Honeywell?'

'There's a lot of short skirts and heels going on at the Randalls offices. I don't like the way he looks at me either. Lewd. Dirty old man in a young man's body. I'll be wearing long dresses and pumps while I'm here.'

'We can swap roles if you like?'

'No, let's stick to the plan. It's what we've told Randall. Besides, I can handle him.'

'If you're sure. So now we come to Honeywell,' I said.

'Been with Randalls ten years, he said. Has he enough ambition to take the plunge and move on? Would he be up to the job of running Ackroyds? How would the existing partners take to being overlooked? It's bound to make waves. Is Ackroyd that desperate?'

'I think he's tired,' I said. 'Any solution to cashing in his partnership will seem good to him. And he's a trusting sort of guy, if I've read him right. Just picked the wrong person in Randall to trust. There's a lot of hidden agenda he hasn't taken into account.'

Cherry sighed. 'Should we try to persuade him not to go ahead? Make out there's something in the accounts?'

'And get sued if someone finds out?' I shook my head. 'Tempting, but too risky. All we can do is get him the best possible price.'

She pulled a face. 'Going to leave a nasty taste in my mouth.'

'Gargle with the money when the invoice gets paid. Day rate plus ten per cent of any frauds found can't be bad.'

'We could always turn down the job?'

'We've signed the contract, Walker. To renege on a contract would be without honour. We have to have a moral code or we're no better than animals.'

'You never cease to surprise me, Shannon. Maybe that's one of the reasons I love you.'

'There're others?'

She shook her head. 'Just give me a decade to think of them.'

CHAPTER FOUR

Anji and I were at Ackroyds at nine the following morning. I was in a dark-blue suit and Anji in her librarian uniform of black suit, loose white blouse and the glasses with false lenses. We announced ourselves to Nancy, who seemed to be running late already, by the way she hardly looked up. I wondered how many visitors she missed while engrossed on her keyboard and monitor. Her space, basically a screened annex off the central working area, was sparsely decorated with shots of Caribbean beaches in the setting sun. I took in the now more familiar bleak surroundings in about thirty seconds as we waited for Ackroyd's secretary to collect us. Beryl arrived, walking slowly, as if arthritis was already taking its toll.

I was starting to think that you had to be post-sixty to qualify for a job here. I hadn't heard the name Beryl for many a year and she was dressed in clothing a cruel person would have called dowdy. Not much change to the outfit when we had met for the first time yesterday: houndstooth dress and jacket that would have been more suitable worn at the hunt on a Sunday morning. There were cat hairs on her shoulder where, I assumed, she couldn't resist a cuddle before setting off. She radiated a caring nature by her smile and extended right hand. There was something about Ackroyds, at least, that made me feel warm.

'I've sorted you out an office,' she said. 'It's not very big considering there's two of you, but at least it's quiet and has a terminal linked to the computer system. I'm afraid it's probably more antiquated to what you're used to. Follow me.'

She led us through a compact central area, where I assumed most of the employees worked, and into a small office partitioned off from the main room. Two chairs were set on one side of a large walnut desk, with a third opposite them. We set up our laptops, and Beryl showed us the water cooler and coffee machine. She then brought in a lady of about forty, ruining Ackroyds' average age of sixty, and introduced her as Sarah Jenkins, accounts supremo and the person from whom we would need the greatest help. We shook hands, told her to call us by our first names, and sat down opposite her.

'How can I help?' she asked. 'Mr Ackroyd said you were to be given every assistance.'

'We'll be doing a quick update from your last audit. We'll start by reconciling your bank account from that time, if you can give us the statements. I take it they are on paper rather than electronic.' It was a fair guess from the business practices I had seen so far.

She nodded, but she did so without making eye contact, staring somewhere in the middle distance. She was not pretty but not unattractive, either. If you had to describe ordinary, then Sarah was the personification of it. Her hair was mousy, her clothes practical and dull, no jewellery. This was a woman who didn't want to stand out from the crowd. I wondered about her home life and whether there was a man there to brighten up her day. Maybe we could get her talking later once we knew her better and got her to relax in our company.

'Can you think of anything else we need, Anji?' I said.

'Staff records,' she guessed correctly, earning a bonus mark. 'Names, functions, salary, partnership records too, dates of birth.'

Jenkins set up our computer terminal, retreated to her office for a moment, and loaded the desk with paper copies of the bank statements. Then she backed out of the room, saying she was popping out for a little while.

When she was out of earshot, I turned to Anji and said, 'Follow her. See where she goes and what she does.'

'Why?' she rightly asked, looking startled.

'Just a feeling. I want to know more about her. If someone was going to commit fraud here, she's in the best place to do it. Humour me.'

While Anji was gone I set up the bank statements as they were on the program and the paper ones beside me for Anji. She would call out the entry on the statements, and I would tick them off on the computer file. There should be no differences.

Anji returned about twenty minutes later.

'Well?' I asked. 'Get up to anything?'

'She's a smoker,' Anji said. 'Lit up as soon as she got outside. Made a phone call. Walked along the road to a delicatessen. Bought a handmade custom sandwich — let's get some for lunch, it looked good — lit another cigarette and walked back. Pretty innocent stuff, all told. Actions of a nicotine addict. Are we going to do this for everyone here?'

'Only those that don't smell right.'

'And she doesn't?'

'Take it from me. She doesn't. We could easily have gone to her office, but she came to us in this little room. I'd like to know why. Here's a test for you. Go into her office on some pretext and look around it. Come back and tell me what you see.'

'What am I looking for?'

'Focus on the walls.'

She frowned. 'That's a bit cryptic.'

'Sometimes cryptic is the best you get.' I waved a hand at the door. 'Shoo.'

And shoo she did.

CHAPTER FIVE

Anji was right. The sandwich bar was good. I had salt beef, English mustard and pickled cucumber on white and Anji had vegan cheese and tomato on brown. We munched happily as we finished checking the firm's bank account. The figures seemed right, but were surprising. The balance in the bank barely moved. They weren't generating any cash: they weren't making any money. We gathered up the papers and decided to pay an unannounced visit to Sarah Jenkins.

Her office was neat and tidy. Not much clutter or paper. No personal photos or anything to give a clue to her personality, her desk clear apart from a computer terminal and printer. On the wall were a collection of postcards of exotic places far and near and a holiday chart, dates in columns and names on the rows. All very methodical. Keep track of holiday taken by each staff member so as not to overpay someone.

'That was quick,' Jenkins said.

'Two heads are better than one,' I replied.

'So do you want the other account next?'

'The other account?' Anji asked, dreading the prospect of more mindless reciting amounts and dates.

'Why, of course. The client account. We have to keep client money separate from our own. It's the rules. No exceptions.'

She went to the top drawer of a grey filing cabinet and removed a stack of papers.

'Here you go,' she said. 'Take your time.'

I moved distractedly to the holiday calendar on her wall, studied it for a bit and then turned back. 'Where's your favourite place to go on holiday?' I asked her.

'Oh, I'm not one for going places. Just take a few days off now and again. Sort out the garden, spring clean the house, have a few day trips to the coast, that sort of thing.'

'Well, I'm sure Mr Ackroyd values your time spent here rather taking two or three weeks in somewhere hot and sunny.' I turned back to her and smiled. 'So, have you got the information I requested on staff, all the full details on each one?'

She walked back to the filing cabinet and took out a transparent folder.

'Names, salaries, dates of birth, length of service, job titles — it's all there. I should remind you that this is extremely sensitive information. I wouldn't want a member of staff to know everyone else's salaries.'

'Quite,' I said. 'You might have a revolt on your hands. Oh, and I need a copy of the last three years' accounts, please.'

'You'd have to ask Beryl for those,' she said, taking a seat behind her desk again. 'Out of my league, I'm afraid.'

'Thanks, Sarah. We'll get out of your hair. Can't guarantee that we won't come back and bother you again, but we'll try not to.' I gave her what I hoped was a reassuring smile and we made our exit.

'What was all that about holidays?' Anji asked when we were back in our room.

'Holidays are revealing. If someone in Accounts is pulling a scam, they wouldn't want anybody to have a chance of discovering it. Go away for a couple of weeks and someone has to do your work. Might discover what you are up to. But if you only go away for two or three days, then everything can be left for your return. All safe and secure.'

'Has anyone ever told you that you have a devious mind?'

'Comes with the job,' I replied, grinning. 'You'll soon acquire the trait. Right, let's look at the personnel information. Come and sit beside me.'

Anji looked over my shoulder as I viewed each page.

'Look at that,' I said, pointing to the figure. 'That's the answer to the riddle. The answer to why the firm isn't making any money. Ackroyd is paying himself a hundred grand and the lion's share of the partnership dividend, leaving little left over. I wonder why the other partners have stayed here.'

'And the job titles,' she said. 'Can I mention that?'

'Well spotted. Tell me.'

'It's the number of admin staff — secretaries, typists, assistants. They're still in the dark ages. A good computer system could cut staff by half. Much of the work must be repetitive. Same documents and just change names and such. I reckon they must treat everything as starting from scratch. Type it all up afresh.'

'You can see why Randall is interested in this. Retire Ackroyd and save a hundred grand. Cut the other staff— on top of the ancient working practices, they could roll much of the admin and accounts work into their existing people — the benefits of synergy. For him, that is. No celebrations here. I bet he's licking his lips. Be an interesting conversation with Cherry tonight.'

Anji took a look at the first page of clients' accounts and whistled. 'Now, this is what I call money,' she said.

The figures were in hundreds of thousands, mostly coming in and out on the same day within an hour of each other. House purchases, I'd presumed. Maybe some corporate work, too. I could check my assumptions tomorrow, when we interviewed the solicitors handling the work.

Just as we were starting to check the accounts, the fire alarm blared out, a high-pitch rhythmic beat. We both sighed and headed for the exit where a small crowd had already developed. Nobody knew quite what to do, and there was a lot of aimless walking around. Most of the staff had initially thought it was a drill, then hoped that it was some form of false alarm. Everybody looked at each other for some guidance.

Anji and I moved to the edge of the gathering. I looked around and realized that someone was missing. Ackroyd. I checked my watch. Just gone three. Cake and Madeira time. Not wishing to re-enter the building, I walked around the corner where the French doors had been open earlier. They were locked now. I peered through the glass and saw Ackroyd slumped forward over his desk. Apparently asleep and impervious to the happening outside.

But was he sleeping? The din of the alarm should have woken him up. I didn't like the look of it. Something was wrong. Against my better judgement, I pushed my way through the crowd and went back inside the offices to Ackroyd's door. It was locked.

Not knowing if Beryl had a spare key and how much time I had before a possible fire could engulf the building, I chose the only option available and ran at the door, barging my shoulder against it with my full weight. The wood of the ancient door shattered and burst open. I rushed up to Ackroyd and shook his shoulder. No movement. I tried to lift him up and then it became clear. Just in case, I felt his neck for a pulse. Nothing.

Ackroyd was dead.

CHAPTER SIX

'Walker,' I said on my phone, from the doorway of the late Ackroyd's office, where I was surveying the scene and trying to make sense of it.

'Shannon.'

'We have a problem.'

'Me, too. You go first.'

'Ackroyd is dead.'

She let out a forgivable expletive.

'Looks like old age caught up with him,' I said.

'Where does that leave us?' she asked.

'In limbo. I suspect that Ackroyd's death won't affect Randall's bid — saves him the trouble of retiring him, but I don't know where that leaves us on the Ackroyds' side. Presumably it means dealing with Ackroyd's estate, and the other partners after that, if they still want to go ahead. You best be first to give Randall the news and see what his reaction is. What was your problem?'

'Randall. He follows me around like a lost sheep, all the time leering and undressing me with his eyes. I was thinking of coming in naked tomorrow and see whether the real thing met his mental picture.'

'It would blow his mind,' I said, feeling a rush of anger sweep over me. This kind of behaviour shouldn't happen these days. At least I knew Cherry could handle it. You wouldn't want to get on the wrong side of her. I winced at the thought. 'I'll be over to talk to Randall as soon as I can get away. Take him through the latest news, and we can work through a plan from there. Must go. The police are here. Love you.'

A tall man in his mid-fifties blocked the light into Ackroyd's office. He had a barrel chest from the effects of too much beer over the years and grey hair receding at the temples. Dressed in an ill-fitting suit of dark grey, he introduced himself as DI Dennis Palmer from the Met and flashed a badge to prove it.

'Who are you and what are you doing here, sir?' he said.

'Nick Shannon. I found the body and guessed you'd want to interview me first.'

'Until we know otherwise, this is now a crime scene, albeit that it looks like natural causes — heart attack, stroke — the autopsy can tell us more,' he said. 'What have you touched in the office?'

'I touched his neck. Felt for a pulse. That's all.'

'What about this glass?' he said, pointing to an empty Madeira glass on the desktop. 'Bit early in the day, isn't it?'

'Ackroyd was an old-fashioned gentleman. Liked to keep up the tradition of afternoon tea. Kept the same routine every day, cake and Madeira at three. He didn't like to drink alone. Should be another glass and a decanter of Madeira in the top drawer of his filing cabinet.'

Palmer walked over to the filing cabinet and peered into the top drawer. 'Decanter, yes, glass, no.'

'Strange,' I said.

'Maybe one got broken,' he said dismissively. 'That must be the explanation.'

'I suppose so.' Something niggled at me, but I dismissed it as being fanciful.

'And this plate?' he asked, looking at a plate on the desk with a half-eaten slice of sponge on it.

'I didn't touch it. I didn't touch anything in the room. Although I was in here yesterday. Must be some of my prints around the place. You'll have my fingerprints on file.'

'I would think so, given your history. Seven years behind bars, wasn't it?'

'That was a long time ago now,' I said. 'But well done for remembering it. You never get prison out of your system, so it's a constant memory for me.'

'I dare say,' he grunted. 'So how did you come to discover the body?'

I recounted the story of the fire alarm and how I had to break Ackroyd's door down.

'So the office door was locked from the inside,' he said. 'The French doors to the courtyard, too? More evidence of heart failure or stroke. No one could have got out.'

'Yes. Both doors locked from the inside. Believe me, I'm an expert with locked doors. That's why I came in the front door.'

Palmer stared at a collection of pens and pencils on the desk. One was out of alignment. He reached across it and put it parallel with the others.

'Should you have done that?' I asked.

'Offends my sense of symmetry. Won't make any difference. Seems like an open-and-shut case to me. Poor man, but at least he died happy with his drink and his cake.'

'If that's all, Inspector, there's a few things I need to sort out.'

'You work here, I presume? So we know where to find you for a statement and any further questions. We'll be here for a while interviewing the staff.'

'I'm only here on a short-term contract. Just a week or so.' I gave him one of my cards. He looked at it and put it in his pocket.

'Forensic accountant,' he said, 'what does that mean?'

'Fraud, basically.'

'So you're an expert on fraud as well as locks. I'll bear that in mind if I ever get fleeced by a locksmith.' He smiled a little at his own joke. A little smile was all that it deserved.

27

I nodded a goodbye at him and left the office. Outside, people were drifting back, rightly assuming that the fire was a false alarm. Anji walked up to me. 'I'll explain later,' I said. 'I need to talk to Beryl first.'

We walked up to Beryl and took her aside.

'I've got some bad news, I'm afraid,' I said. 'Roger is dead.'

She crumpled, swayed from side to side. I caught her as she passed out and carried her into the main office and sat her in the first chair in the room. A small crowd began to gather.

'Give her some air!' I shouted. 'Someone get a glass of water and make a cup of hot sweet tea.' Brandy would have been better, I thought, but needs must. I lowered her head to between her knees. She began to come round.

'Roger?' she said. 'Did I hear you say that he was dead?'

'Yes, I'm so sorry. Seems like heart failure. It would have been peaceful.'

'Twenty years,' she said. 'Twenty years I've been working for him. It can't be all over. Not like this. He was due to retire. To do all those things he hadn't done because of work. It's so unfair. He was such a lovely man.'

A tall man in a black pinstripe suit came over. 'What's going on?' he said.

It was then I realized that no one else knew what was going on either. 'Roger is dead,' I said. 'Heart attack, stroke, something like that. The police are here and will want to talk to everyone. Best if they all keep away from his office until the Scenes of Crime officers have finished.'

'David Baker,' he said. 'Partner. You must be Shannon. I'll take over from here. First thing is to get Beryl home. If the police want to talk to her, they can do it tomorrow.'

'I can take her home,' said Anji. 'Especially if I get to drive the Beamer.'

I sighed, now regretting driving in that day. 'Remember it's an M3. It's a powerful car. Take care of it.'

'Brmmm brmmm,' she said.

CHAPTER SEVEN

Baker organized the melee of staff into a tight group in the main office and made his announcement. I stood at the back of the room out of everyone's way. I could sense mixed emotions — fear and suspicion. The fear was for their jobs, their patriarch had gone after so many years. I was sure the suspicion was that my arrival had put excess pressure on Ackroyd and led to his death. Not a great environment to carry out our task, but then, would we have a task at all come the following morning?

In the background, officers in white overalls did what they had to do efficiently. A female officer went round the staff and took all their contact details for statements in the morning, should they be necessary.

At a loss until Anji got back, I went into Beryl's empty office and took in her working environment. It was neat and tidy — Palmer would have loved it — everything in its right place. There was a simple desk with a laptop and two large filing cabinets in grey steel. I sat myself down at her desk and contemplated what to do. I tried to think positively. There could well be a change of taskmasters ahead. What would happen to a firm that was majority-owned by a dead man?

There would need to be a valuation by someone for dealing with Ackroyd's executors. What would be the price of Ackroyd's shares?

I went over to the steel cabinets, where — I hoped — Beryl had filed away the information I would need. The hanging folders in the filing cabinets were labelled in black ink under plastic protectors and made my task easy. I extracted the copies of the last three years' accounts and a six-monthly update for the current year: this seemed to be the way they did things.

As I was carrying them back to her desk, Baker came in.

'What do you think you are doing?' he said.

'Just getting some files to work on the current state of the business.'

'Bit presumptuous, aren't we?' he snapped.

I shrugged. 'Nothing else to do.'

'We are convening a meeting between us and the executor of Roger's estate tomorrow at eleven in the morning. You best be there.'

He left the office, giving me a scowl from the doorway.

I looked at the room again. There was a small cupboard to the right of a window. I opened it up. There inside was a spare bottle of Madeira. Nothing else of interest. I went back to the filing cabinets and opened them all in turn and looked inside.

Interesting.

No second glass.

I walked to the kitchen and checked there. Small worktop clear. Draining rack empty except for a few mugs.

Where on earth could it have gone?

* * *

Anji returned, and we compared notes on the happening in the last hour. She had left after a female police officer arrived to sit with Beryl while she recovered from the shock.

'What was her house like?' I asked.

Anji gave me a puzzled look and answered. 'Typical three-bedroom semi in the suburbs — that's what took me so long. Nice street away from the hustle and bustle.'

'And inside?'

'A little dated. Too many knick-knacks for my liking. Dusting must be hell. Why do you ask?'

'Any signs that she might be living beyond her means?'

'You don't suspect Beryl to be doing some scam, surely?'

'No, I don't think she's the type, but always worth checking. Come on, let's pack up and go. There's nothing else to do here.'

We gathered up the accounts and the bank statements for the client account and headed out of the main office. We were about to pass the reception area when I stopped in front of Nancy. 'Any strangers in here today?' I asked.

'I already told the policeman.' She frowned. 'Nothing unusual. A couple of clients in this morning to sign documents, but no one in the afternoon. Pretty quiet until the fire alarm went off. Hard to keep track after that.'

We walked into the porch and I stopped. There was one of those little boxes fixed to the wall. Fire alarm. Someone had taken the attached hammer and broken the glass. That was what had triggered the alarm to go off. Not a false alarm, after all. The original makes more sense. But, the question was, who?

CHAPTER EIGHT

I told Anji she might as well get off home, take the accounts with her and get Norman to start working through things with her. I left the Beamer in the car park at Temple and took a black cab to Randalls. Cherry was already sitting in Randall's office when I arrived. True to her word, she was wearing a long dress in an ethnic print, like they wore in the sixties and a pair of low-heeled squaw boots in suede with a fringe of leather tassels. As ever, she looked beautiful. I couldn't imagine Randall had changed his attitude towards her. I would be playing second fiddle.

I took the spare seat opposite his desk and looked him in the eye. He looked at me briefly and then shifted his gaze to Cherry.

'So Ackroyd is dead,' he said. 'Do you have any details that might help me put this sad event in perspective?'

'He died just after three while having his cake and Madeira,' I said. 'The police are putting it down as a natural death — a stroke or heart attack. Would seem to fit the bill, as both doors were locked from the inside.'

'What's the reaction of the staff?' he asked.

'Too early to tell,' I said. 'There's some pretty long-serving staff there. It will hit them hard. They'll be worried about their future, too, now that their friendly grandfather has gone. Beryl's been working for him for twenty years. I think their second thought, after sadness, must be about who takes over. Will they even still have a job when the dust settles?'

'And do *we* still have a job?' said Cherry. 'How does this affect our contract?'

'Sad though I am about Roger's death, nothing has changed,' he said, addressing Cherry. 'I want this takeover to go ahead as planned. The only difference is that I will be dealing with the executors of his estate instead of Roger himself.'

'Who presumably will be anxious to sell,' I said. 'The only use of the shares will be any dividend when it's paid out at the end of the year. Whatever that turns out to be. With good accountancy, that could be made very small and still allow the partners to get their hands on the money.'

'That's exactly what I would do in their position,' he said. 'Nothing illegal there.'

'May not be illegal, but it would be immoral,' I said.

'Nick has a strict moral code,' Cherry said.

'Then you won't get far,' he said. 'Take a lesson from me, Shannon. It's a dog-eat-dog world out there. There's no room for morality. Morals are a weakness. Something invented by the weak to keep the strong in check.'

I resisted gritting my teeth. 'Well,' I said, as calmly as possible. 'Someday I hope to prove you wrong.'

* * *

'Drink. I need a drink,' Cherry said as we entered the first-floor lounge area where Norman, Anji, and Morag were regrouping. I went straight to the drinks cabinet and the fridge and made a large G&T for Cherry and a vodka and fresh orange juice for myself. Everyone else had already started on sundowners.

'That sort of day?' Norman said to her.

'You wouldn't believe it. Randall,' she spat, 'what a jerk.'

'Discuss,' I said.

'He was hitting on me all the time. I don't know how the female staff cope. I did notice that they're all young attractive women working there. It's like a harem. He kept making some sort of excuse for squeezing past me in the corridor.'

'Opposite end of the spectrum at Ackroyd's,' I said. 'Hardly anyone under the age of fifty, and that's being kind. I feel a cull brewing if the merger goes ahead. How do you think he really feels about Ackroyd's death?'

'I wouldn't say cock-a-hoop.' Cherry paused. 'No, I *would* say cock-a-hoop. Reckons he can strike a deal more easily with Ackroyd's estate. He'd already written off most of Roger Ackroyd's clients. They were dwindling anyway as they got even older and died off. Thinks he can pick up the firm for a pittance now.'

'Good timing for Ackroyds and for Randalls,' I said slowly. 'The middle ground is disappearing. To survive nowadays you either have to be a one-man-band or big enough to cover the whole market. Give it another five years and there won't be any medium-sized law firms anymore.'

'That's the way of the world,' said Norman, who was sitting next to Morag on one of the sofas drinking an expensive red wine. Anji, for some strange reason, had opted to sit on the floor in a crossed-leg yoga position. She was drinking a white wine in such small sips that the one glass would last the whole evening.

'So, where do we stand?' asked Morag. 'Job on or off? Should I start bringing forward some appointments?' Morag was our everyday girl Friday — woman Friday, I suppose — and ran the whole office like a military campaign. We'd be lost without her.

'We won't know anything about Ackroyds before the meeting at 11 a.m. tomorrow. Continuing with the merger would be the sensible thing.'

'But when do clients do the sensible thing?' Norman said before asking, 'Any fraud of interest?'

'We found a woman who doesn't take more than three days' holiday at a time,' said Anji, having learnt at least one lesson today. She really was a bright button.

'Ah hah,' said Norman. 'Like the sound of it. What job does she do?'

'Accounts,' I said.

'Ah hah again,' said Norman. 'Should we investigate her? We could get Arthur to follow her around. Look into her lifestyle and spending habits?'

I nodded, and Morag said, 'I'll call him tomorrow.'

'I'll get her home address from the personnel files,' said Anji.

Arthur had been my cellmate in Brixton where I had been incarcerated while on remand. He was an ex-wrestler who had taught me how to survive in prison and now functioned as part of our machine when needed. He had been falsely imprisoned for collecting debts that didn't exist on behalf of a seedy man who ran a minor protection racket. Now, he worked as a door steward — bouncer — picking up jobs on a short-term contract where he could. He was six-foot-five and built like a rugby player. No one got past Arthur; he was a one-man scrum.

'So the police reckon Ackroyd's death was natural causes?' asked Norman.

'Yes, and I don't like it,' I said. 'There's the mystery of the missing wine glass. Then there's the fire alarm incident. Someone smashed the glass and set off the alarm on purpose. Too much of a coincidence. The fact that both doors were locked from the inside suits the police theory of death by natural causes, but we know how easy it is to open and close a badly fitting door. The door to the courtyard was locked, but old. Could be some give in it.'

'Have the police ruled out suicide?' said Norman.

'It's not an option they have considered so far,' I said. 'I have doubts about the officer running the case. Anal retentive. Couldn't resist putting the pens on Ackroyd's desk parallel to one another. Maybe up for retirement and looking for a quiet life. Open-and-shut case as far as he was concerned.'

'Whatever the partners at Ackroyds decide to do, they'll need a valuation, surely,' said Cherry. 'My guess is Ackroyd's estate will need one, too. Set an independent price for its shares.'

'Makes sense,' said Norman. 'We can't rule that out. My guess is we'll still have to complete the project.'

Anji piped up. 'Do you think Ackroyd's death is related to our investigation of their finances? Does someone want us to stop doing what we have been engaged to do? That would be interesting.'

'May I remind you,' I said, 'that the last job that was "interesting" almost got me killed.'

'Well,' said Norman, 'to be fair, you do seem to have a history of dead bodies following you around.'

'Only one,' I said defensively. 'Well, two if you go back a ways.'

'Oh, I almost forgot,' Morag said. 'Toddy sent this parcel for you, Cherry.'

Toddy had been a brilliant head chef in Chelmsford, where he was serving a sentence for forgery. On his release, Norman had set him up in a restaurant which was now so successful that it was booked up weeks in advance. Toddy specialized in the best ingredients cooked simply, so the flavours shone through.

Morag got up and went to fetch a small parcel from the kitchen worktop. She presented it to Cherry.

'Well, I wonder what this is?' said Cherry, tearing off the wrapping.

Inside was a small box.

She opened the box and took out a small wallet.

Inside the wallet was . . . a police badge and warrant card with details of the holder. Forged, of course. And to perfection; that went without saying.

'Toddy reckoned it might come in handy at times,' said Norman.

'What kind of business have you got me into, Shannon?' Cherry said, looking at me with wide eyes.

'Back to Anji's theory,' I said. 'You never know when times might get interesting.'

'Amen,' said Norman.

CHAPTER NINE

The next morning, I told Anji to take her time and meet me at ten a.m. for preparations for the meeting to decide the future of Ackroyds. I headed off with Cherry to Randalls. It deserved more investigation. The person who looked after the accounts function there held the title of 'financial controller', and she was about as pleased to see us as Nigel Honeywell had been the previous day — which is to say, not very.

Her name was Tracy Watkins. An average height for Randalls, five nine or so, was wearing the regulation short skirt, black in this case, and a tight white top which emphasized her — potentially enhanced — figure. She had green eyes and a Roman nose that would probably be next for cosmetic surgery. Her shoes, of course, were heels: what else did they wear at Randalls? I shook my head at what seemed to be an inappropriate yet expected dress code.

Her office was partitioned off from the main working space with thick walls, evidently so that when she talked about finance she couldn't be overheard. There was a pinboard on one wall which had the inevitable holidays' calendar and postcards from all around the world — she must be popular with the other staff to amass such a collection. She didn't offer us a seat but we sat down anyway, hoping to annoy her. It worked.

'I don't have much time,' she said brusquely, looking at her watch.

'A cog in something turning?' I said, reciting the theme.

'Everyone is always busy here,' Cherry agreed, watching Tracy. 'Seems like a lot of unpaid overtime occurring.'

'Needs must,' she said. 'So how can I help you?'

'We do all the things an auditor does . . .' I said.

'But even quicker,' said Cherry. 'It's important, though, to understand the staff and their work practices.'

'Practice makes perfect,' Tracy said, to prove she was quick on the draw.

'Do you handle the accounts function on your own?' Cherry asked.

'I used to,' she said, 'but with all the acquisitions, the workload has grown over the years, and I now have an assistant who helps me or covers for me for holidays and sickness. How much more work there will be with the acquisition of Ackroyds is anyone's guess. I expect, though, to still be in charge of the function. Ackroyds, so the grapevine tells me, is still in the dark ages. We have a state-of-the-art computer system — I doubt that they could adapt.'

'Do you feel threatened at all by who might move over from Ackroyds?' I asked.

She smiled tightly. 'With all due modesty, I'm good at my job. I'd go so far as to say that I'm invaluable to the practice. They wouldn't want to lose me or give me any cause for dissatisfaction. I can walk at any time and get another job if I wanted.'

'What keeps you here then?' said Cherry.

'It pays well. I doubt that any firm could match what I'm on at the moment.'

'But there's more to it than that,' I said.

'How is it that only solicitors can become partners?' she said. 'I want to break that glass ceiling. As I said, I think I'm invaluable. The practice would be lost without me. I'll get there one day. Maybe with the acquisition of Ackroyds, the time will be ripe for staking my claim. I haven't done too bad for someone who hasn't got a degree. I had good A levels in maths, economics and business studies — didn't see much point in another three years of study at university running up debts.'

'Let's get to the money,' Cherry said. 'Who can access the accounts and make payments?'

'Me, my assistant when I'm not around and, of course, the computer. Before making a payment, the payee's details have to be put into the program. It checks that the receiving account actually exists and that the right name corresponds to that account. I'm positive you won't find any holes in the system,' she concluded firmly. 'You won't find any chance of fraud here.'

'A determined fraudster will always find a way to beat the system,' I said, 'but, granted, you seem to have reduced the odds. Cherry will go through the system in more detail later.'

'Let me demonstrate,' Tracy said. She turned the monitor around so that Cherry and I could see it. 'The name of your business — the one where the money should go.'

'Shannon Investigations Limited.'

She typed that into a field on the screen. 'You're already in the system, since you submitted your first invoice. Now, watch what happens if I type in a false account number.'

The screen blinked and brought up a window that said the name and account number did not match.

'See what happens if I type in the proper account number.'

I gave her our account details. She typed in the account number and sort code.

The screen opened up a new window and asked for the amount to pay.

'So you see,' she said proudly, 'there's no chance of a payment going to the wrong payee. If a fraudster wanted to divert money to his or her account, it wouldn't work.'

'Impressive,' I said. 'What if you simply added a false payee — a new account, say — with a new account number and a corresponding new correct name?'

She was quiet for a moment. 'That couldn't happen,' she eventually said. 'The only people that can input a new payee is myself and my assistant.'

'I rest my case,' I said.

'I trust my assistant,' she replied coldly.

'Trust can be a double-edged sword,' I pressed. 'For instance, Randall obviously trusts you, but that could backfire on him if you decided to commit a fraud. There's a Latin phrase. *Quis custodiet custodes?* Or, "Who guards the guards?"'

'I've been doing this job for five years,' she said. 'If I wanted to steal money from the firm, I could have done it before now.'

'Or maybe you're waiting for the big kill,' Cherry said. 'Like the large sums that need to be paid to Ackroyds. What if I set up a payee called "Ackroyd's" — Ackroyds with an apostrophe. No one then would blink an eye. A million gone by a few taps on a keyboard.'

'But,' she protested, 'I would never do that. It's not all about the money. That would be life-changing, in many ways. On the plus side, I could afford that apartment in Marbella I've set my heart on. On the negative side, I'd spend the rest of my life looking over my shoulder for some policeman to show up and take it all away.'

'Just a hypothetical case,' I said. 'I wasn't implying anything about your honesty, but you must see the weakness of the system. At the end of the day, it's all down to people, and people have a way of getting around barriers. It's worth thinking about, in terms of the latitude your assistant has and the opportunities that provides.'

'Well, thanks very much for that,' she said frostily. 'I now have to watch carefully every move my assistant makes. You sure do know how to make a person feel edgy.'

'In terms of my job here, working on the Randalls side,' Cherry said, 'you are the most important person, so don't take anything that Nick says personally. He just likes to show that he's clever. Let's have a clean sheet. Start afresh. Friends?'

'Why not?' she said. 'Friends.'

'I think that we can let Nick go — he's done enough harm already,' Cherry said, shooting me a look. 'Rest assured I won't be so critical.'

I slunk away with my tail between my legs.

* * *

'Well, you certainly knew how to rain on her parade,' Cherry said, when we were back in our allotted room.

'I thought we were playing good cop, bad cop,' I said. 'She'll confide in you now. That's the way it works.'

'You shattered her confidence.' Cherry frowned. 'She is going to be watching every move her assistant makes in the future.'

'And so she should. The system, despite its power, has the prospect of being leaky. Randall should be worried, too. Get one phoney invoice into the system, and the door is open to the floodgates. I could do it tomorrow, and then empty the bank account. We haven't even talked about the client account yet, and that's where the real money goes through.'

'Granted,' Cherry said. 'Okay, forget about the system for the moment. What did we learn about her?'

'She's conflicted. She wants the takeover to go through because she would have more responsibility, get a salary rise and a bigger job — plus the better chance of getting that promotion to partner that she most definitely wants. Yet she's worried, because she doesn't know who would be coming in from Ackroyds. Would that person be running things?'

'And the balance of probabilities?' Cherry asked.

'Go for the takeover, play a waiting game. That works, apart from one thing.'

'And that is?'

'Is she defrauding the firm already and afraid we might uncover it?'

'Time will tell,' Cherry said.

'It always does,' I said. 'It always does.'

* * *

Anji and I met up at Ackroyds at ten a.m. and spent the next hour before the meeting looking over the accounts. I explained the intricacies of balance sheets and profits-and-loss statements where income and expenditure were itemized by the most important categories. They merely confirmed our conclusions that the practice wasn't making any money. Not a good negotiating position for a merger or a share sale.

One thing that stood out was the amount of money spent on 'entertaining' for a business that didn't really warrant wining and dining clients. That would need some investigating to see if anyone was profligate . . . providing, of course, that we still had a job in the afternoon.

In the background, I could see Inspector Palmer and a uniformed male officer making their rounds of the office staff, taking statements and fingerprints one by one. At some stage, being the person who found the body, he would get to me. Not that I could add to what I had told him the previous afternoon.

Beryl entered the room bearing coffee for Anji and me.

'Thank you, Anji, for taking me home,' she said. 'It was such a shock but I know what a silly billy I was, it had to come some time. None of us are getting any younger. John Samson said I could take some time off, but I would rather try to get back to normal — getting back on the horse, you know? I'm over the shock now and would like to be useful. There must be so much to do.'

I wondered if she had thought of the likely prospect of being made redundant. With Ackroyd gone, where did she stand? Surplus to requirements? There wouldn't be much call for Madeira and sponge cake anymore.

'Did the police ask you any questions while they were looking after you?' I asked Beryl.

'They were kind, but I think they were trying to see if I had an alibi. What was I doing when the fire alarm went off? When was the last time I had seen him? That kind of stuff. Pretty persistent. I hope they don't think I was involved in some way with Roger's death. Still, if, as it seems, it was a heart attack or stroke, then I suppose there's nothing to investigate? What a pretty pickle.'

* * *

Given that Ackroyd's office was still out of bounds, cordoned off by tape, there were three people across the table in a small room prepared for the meeting: John Samson and David Baker, the partners, one of which was soon to become senior partner, and a homely woman in her sixties who could only be Ackroyd's widow. She was dressed in a below-the-knee RAF-blue dress over a white blouse that made her look very much like a hospital matron. I found I kept looking for one of those upside-down watches.

Samson, neatly trimmed beard and in his early thirties, was average height with brown hair and green eyes. He was soberly dressed in what I now knew was the solicitor uniform of a dark suit, although this one was too loose around his thin body. For some strange reason — medical, presumably — he was wearing glasses with a pale-yellow tint.

Baker, mid-fifties with receding hair and brown eyes and a generously cut suit which failed to hide a tubby body. The only break from convention was a blue tie with a yellow elephant motif. Rebel without a cause, eh?

Prior to the meeting, I had briefed Anji. She was to draw a table plan with the three of them marked in their position at the table and make notes on style of dress, mannerisms and body language, as if she was sizing up players in a game of poker.

Baker took control, making introductions and starting the meeting with a homily to Ackroyd for his kind patriarchal leadership over the years. Mrs Ackroyd — Fiona, we were told — remained stoic and doodled on a pad on the table before her as though she had little interest in proceedings. Playing it cool?

She was invited to speak by Baker. 'Mr Shannon and Miss . . .' she paused.

'Anji, just Anji.'

'The shares are no use to me,' Fiona said. 'They will be an unnecessary burden. I wish to sell at an equitable price — that is to be your role, Mr Shannon. An independent outsider setting a price fair to all.'

Baker nodded. Samson was impassive. As a displacement activity, he stroked his beard.

'So,' I said, 'you still want to go ahead with the merger with Randalls?'

'Possibly,' she said cryptically.

'Let me explain,' said Baker. 'We are considering an option of a management buyout, maintaining our independence.'

'Even though,' I said, 'the middle ground is fast disappearing. Going alone may be a dangerous strategy in the longer term. You'll gradually lose clients to the big boys until it won't be profitable to carry on.'

'We had thought of that,' said Baker. 'We were thinking of modernizing the practice, investing for the future and promoting some of the senior staff to partners. Start afresh.'

'Sentimentally,' Fiona said, 'I would like to retain the legacy of the past, but, realistically, I want the best price for my shares and I don't want to see Roger's heritage given away for a pittance.'

'You do realize,' I said to Baker, 'that modernization will mean redundancies. Is that to be Roger's heritage?'

'Give us a fair price for the shares either to buy from Fiona or to merge with Randalls, and we can consider which is the right path for us.'

Samson nodded, his only contribution to the meeting so far.

'Our contract with you still stands,' said Baker. 'We would be grateful for a swift conclusion. Everything needs to be tidied up as quickly as possible. There's probate to consider as well — Fiona needs a value for that. Do it as fast as you can, Mr Shannon. We don't want any loose ends.'

* * *

Although Beryl's coffee was acceptable given the equipment at her disposal — a kettle, basically — Anji and I were desperate for some real espresso, so we gathered up our notes from the meeting and entered the chain coffee shop nearest to Ackroyds' offices. We sat in a quiet corner away from other customers, sipping pleasurably.

'What did you make of that?' I said to Anji.

She consulted her notes and said, 'Strange. I can understand Mrs Ackroyd's position. She doesn't want to be lumbered with shares of little value. But what can one assume about Samson's personality? He didn't say a word. I wondered whether he was sulking. Defensive body language — arms crossed across his chest. Didn't look us in the eye. And the tinted glasses? Are they something to do with his sight, or just an affectation.'

'And Baker?'

'I think his goal will be top dog in a new Ackroyds — maybe that was why Samson was sulking. Baker took control of the meeting and only surrendered that to Fiona Ackroyd for her opening speech. Be interesting to know about his history.'

'And the elephant tie?'

'Seemed out of character.'

'Just one thing to bear in mind.'

'Which is?'

'Elephants never forget.'

CHAPTER TEN

Palmer and the male constable were waiting for us when we returned to Ackroyds. He did not look a happy man. He was red in the face, and his barrel chest was puffed out ready to burst.

'Where have you been?' he shouted at both of us. 'I've been looking all over for you. You're the last ones to be interviewed and fingerprinted. I need to get this incident straightened out — shipshape and Bristol fashion — before we leave here for a while.'

'Just out for a coffee, Inspector Palmer,' I said. 'Not cooking up any plots to distract you or muddy the waters.'

'Right,' he snapped. 'Let's get on. Fingerprints first. I'll take yours, as well as your assistant's, just in case anything has changed.'

'Is that possible?' I asked. 'I thought a fingerprint was for life.'

'Can't be too careful. Everything in its place and suchlike.'

The constable produced a paper template and laid it on the desk of our little room, opened an inkpad and took Anji's prints and then my own. Palmer offered us nothing to wipe the ink off.

'So, tell me,' he said, 'about your movements yesterday afternoon.'

'In here working with Anji when the fire alarm sounded. Initially, we didn't know what the procedure was. Thought it best to get out so we joined the other staff in the courtyard.'

'And?'

'I realized that Roger Ackroyd was missing and went to look through the French doors — didn't think it was sensible to go back into the offices with the alarm still going. Saw him asleep at his desk, or that's what I assumed. Banged on the doors, but no reaction. It was then I resorted to going inside and trying his office door. Broke the door down. Saw him immobile and checked for a pulse. I knew we had to call for an ambulance and, just in case, yourselves at the police. End of story.'

'But is it?' Palmer said 'Let's go back to the fire alarm. Not a routine test. Agreed? So someone set it off deliberately.'

'A bit after finding Ackroyd dead, I saw that the glass on the box had been shattered. It was then that I started to wonder about the motive of the person who set off the alarm and the coincidence. But you were sure that Ackroyd's death was natural causes. Dismissed anything sinister. Surely, you knew what you were doing. Didn't think any more of it.'

'You're an expert on locks, you said?'

'I was before I was locked up but prison made me more so. In there, your daily routine is run by locks. Locked in your cell, unlocked for a morning wash and shave. Back to your cell, locked again. Unlocked for exercise. And so it goes.'

'So what did you make of the room with both of the entrances and exits locked when you broke in?'

'That there was nothing at that stage to indicate other than Ackroyd had locked both of them himself.'

'As an expert, as you claim, do you know how someone could get out, then lock the doors from the inside?'

'Well, the French doors were old, ill-fitting. Big gap where they met. Susceptible to locking from the outside.'

'You best show me. Follow me.'

We walked through the office and crouched under the police tape and into Ackroyd's inner sanctum. I unlocked the French doors and pulled them wide open. I locked the right-hand door, went outside and took both doors in my hands. I slowly pulled the doors together and, at the right point, slid the lock a little into the start of the other door. Then, together, I pulled them tight. The lock slid into the fixing and both doors came together. With a final pull, the doors clicked into place.

'Well,' said Palmer after he had let me back in to the office, 'how could someone unaccustomed to locks know the trick you did?'

'Read a lot of cosy crime, maybe, or watched the afternoon mystery slots? But, of course, there is another way.'

'Which is?'

'You use a lock picker. Pick the lock from the outside to gain entry. Do the deed and lock the door again from the outside with the same picker.'

'You see my problem, Mr Shannon,' he said accusingly. 'You're the first to arrive on the scene, and you know how to unlock and lock doors from the outside. Makes you my prime suspect.'

'Prime suspect of what?' I asked. 'I thought there was no crime, just natural death. That's what you said yesterday.'

'Ah, that was yesterday.'

'And what's changed?'

'I now have the autopsy report. There were traces of strychnine in Ackroyd's stomach. Not a natural death, after all. He was poisoned.'

Silence. This was more complex than we had thought.

'Now what do you have to say about that, Mr Shannon?'

'I have an alibi — Anji can corroborate my movements.'

He took off his glasses and wiped them on a fresh tissue from his pocket that he unfolded, used and refolded. I doubted that they needed a clean — he was just leaving a space to build the tension.

'Not a great alibi. She's your employee; you could have put pressure on her to back up your story. Death by strychnine would not have been instantaneous,' he said. 'It takes a few minutes, apparently, to get into his bloodstream and have the full effect. You could have poisoned him, gone through the French doors, locked them like you showed us, back to the front of the building and set off the fire alarm. We only have your word that Ackroyd was dead when you broke down the door. It could have been death a few minutes after your entry, yet before you called for the police and an ambulance. Solved — neat and tidy.'

'But what would have been my motive? I only met Roger Ackroyd yesterday.'

'You could have been paid to do it by Randalls — make it easy to pick up Ackroyd's shares cheaply.'

'Doesn't it all sound a bit fanciful?' said Anji, coming to my defence. 'Sounds to me like you're fishing around to put the blame on Nick, so you can wrap up your inquiry. Done and dusted.'

'Is this your first murder?' I asked Palmer.

'Not my first, but will be the last. I retire in a month's time. Twenty-two years' service; I don't want my successor to inherit a mess.'

'Is that solely your aim?' said Anji coldly. 'How about leaving no stone unturned? Do some proper detective work.'

Palmer glanced at Anji whose face was set. You don't mess with her. Palmer had picked the wrong fight.

'Mr Shannon was the one who pointed out the missing wine glass,' Palmer said. 'Throw suspicion on to someone else, I reckon. Here's how I see it. You join Ackroyd for Madeira and cake. You manage to put strychnine into his glass — the bitter taste of the strychnine being masked by the strong flavour of the wine. Ackroyd wouldn't notice any difference from his usual tipple. You wait till he starts to die, take his wine glass so the poison would not be evident and pocket it. The other wine glass — yours — you wipe and rub with his fingers and leave on the desk knowing that it would not test positive for the poison. You can see how it looks to me.'

'Any evidence would be purely circumstantial,' I said. 'What fingerprint evidence do you have?'

'Your prints were found on the desk.'

'Because I had tea with him yesterday,' I said calmly. 'I told you that.'

'You could have set that up. Had murder in mind already.'

'And what about the fire alarm? Any prints on that or the hammer?'

'Wiped clean. No prints at all.'

'So where do we go from here?' I asked.

'To the station for more questions and everything recorded on tape. I'll spare you the handcuffs.'

'Do you want me to call a lawyer?' said Anji.

'Call Martin. He'll clear this up in no time. Martin has helped us in the past. Morag will have his number. I'll leave you to drive the Beamer back.'

'Not all bad then,' she said.

CHAPTER ELEVEN

Palmer took me to Holborn police station and led me into an interview room with the recording equipment already set up. He sat one side of a small table with the female sergeant next to him, her cap off and brown hair scraped back and secured by two plastic clips. On the opposite side of the table were two hard-backed chairs where I sat, the empty seat ready for Martin when he arrived.

There was a fresh page in a pad and two ballpoint pens — one black, the other red — on the table in front of Palmer. I reached across and took the fresh page of the pad and both pens and scribbled on the virgin page. I slid the pad back, upside down to Palmer, and put both pens at acute angles on top. Palmer's face went red again. He tore off the page on which I had scribbled, crumpled it up and tossed it towards a steel waste-paper bin which he missed. He straightened both pens and sighed, everything neat and tidy again. The sergeant hid a smile and started the recording equipment.

Palmer did the usual preamble of the time and those present then turned his attention to me.

'You know why you are here?' he said.

'I will make no comment until my lawyer arrives.'

'Something to hide, Shannon?'

'No comment.'

'What do you know of strychnine?'

I leaned back in the chair and put my feet on the table and my arms behind my head. 'No comment.'

'So you knew that Ackroyd had an afternoon session with the wine and cake?'

'No comment.'

Palmer's face went red again. A vein started to throb on his neck.

Martin arrived, debonair in grey trousers and a dark-blue blazer with gold buttons. 'Anji has briefed me,' he said. 'I'll handle this from now on.'

He sat down, opened his briefcase and took a set of manila folders. He placed them on the desk in a clutter. Palmer looked at them, obviously itching to straighten them up and creating a neat pile.

'What evidence do you have against my client?' Martin said.

'I can place him at the scene of the crime.'

'Along with how many others?'

'He discovered the body.'

'Well, someone had to. As I understand it my client was doing an altruistic act, trying to save Mr Ackroyd from a fire.'

'He knows how to lock doors from the outside.'

'Let me answer that one, Martin,' I said.

'Go ahead,' he replied.

'No comment.'

'I think it's time that this charade was over,' Martin said. 'Do you have any evidence to detain my client further?'

Palmer paused.

'I'll take that as a no, then.' Martin stood up. 'This interview is over.'

I rose and pressed the button on the recording equipment.

'Any more detaining of my client,' Martin warned, 'and I will charge you with harassment. I understand you're coming up to retirement, inspector. I suspect you would like to leave with an unblemished record, rather than finish up in a courtroom. I suggest you look for the real culprit for the murder, rather than interfering with the work of an innocent man. Goodbye, inspector.'

The sergeant opened the door, leaving Palmer red-faced. I could sense his eyes searing into my back. What fun we had had.

* * *

Martin and I walked to the coffee shop for an espresso fix.

'Thanks for turning up so quickly, Martin,' I said.

'I didn't feel I could cross Anji. Pretty persuasive, with a hint of threat. Like she could come round and squeeze my balls 'til future children were an impossibility.'

I laughed grimly before saying, 'While we're here, can I pick your brains?'

'Won't take long,' he said.

'What do you know of Ackroyds? What do the jungle drums say?'

'That old man Ackroyd was past it. Few of his clients remain and the work for them was done adequately by a junior. Note the word *adequately*. Ackroyd should have retired years ago. He bled the firm dry. I don't like talking ill of the dead, but they won't miss him.'

'What will happen to the firm now that Ackroyd is dead?'

'Dead man walking,' he said. 'It's over for the firm as we know it.'

I got more coffee while I pondered the fate of the people at Ackroyds.

'And how about Randall?' I asked, as we stirred more sugar into our coffee — actually, Martin had a sweetener, but I didn't hold that against him.

'Randall,' Martin said. 'Richard Randall. Known as Tricky Dicky. Specialist in tax avoidance. Knows the ins and outs of minimizing and delaying tax. Plays close to the wire. Sought after for his skills.'

'Anything else said about him? Like, as a person?'

'Different kettle of fish to Ackroyd. Other end of the spectrum. Treats the staff like slaves. They're supposed to start early. Work till they're finished, whatever time that is. But he pays well, so the staff suffer and stay.'

'Do you feel threatened by a firm like Randalls?'

Martin shook his head. 'We're a pretty big firm ourselves. Strong enough to win and keep clients. Everything done professionally — I think Randall cuts corners. But he'll keep hoovering up small firms until he is a major force in the profession.'

'What would you do in my position?'

'Advise Randall to buy. It's not all about profit. From what I hear, Ackroyds owns the premises in Temple. Must be worth a fortune. I don't know whether it is owned by Roger Ackroyd personally or by the firm — that might be worth checking out. It'll make a huge difference to the value of the merger — or, more accurately takeover, because that's what it will be. Randall will cut staff and asset-strip. The place will never be the same again.'

'Sounds like I have to suppress my conscience,' I said. 'The solicitors will be kept and indoctrinated into the Randall's way; the administrative staff will be cut to the bone.'

'As I said,' Martin replied. 'Dead man walking. The ethos of the firm will die.'

CHAPTER TWELVE

When work was over, we assembled for dinner at Toddy's. The place was full and the atmosphere was calm, both staff and diners contented. Usually, whatever restaurant you go to, there is a couple having an argument. Not so at Toddy's; it's been responsible for many a relationship make-up rather than break-up.

We sat at a round table that Toddy always kept for Norman — the owner's privilege. Drinks arrived swiftly — mine was a vodka and fresh orange juice, got to keep up your vitamin C intake — with a bucket of ice for the white wine and a bottle of Pomerol opened and decanted to breathe. We perused the menu and I chose one of the specials of the day — swordfish with flageolet beans and chunky triple-cooked chips. There was a good range of choices, so making one's mind up and ordering took a while. The philosophy was fine ingredients cooked simply so the flavours sung through. We unfolded our blue napkins onto our laps. All very civilized. Especially welcome after the events of the last couple of days. Nothing like a death to sharpen one's appetite. I jest.

'I have a plan,' I said.

There was a collective groan.

'Oh God,' Cherry said. 'Not another plan. What are we in for now?'

'I'm trying to rid you of the problem of Randall,' I protested, 'or at least defuse it for a while.'

'And?'

'I will come to Randalls tomorrow.'

'And how will that help?'

'I will bring Anji.'

'Ah,' Cherry said.

'In full feisty mode.'

'Back to the biker boots, is it?' said Anji.

'And the skater skirt and the tank top.' It was the outfit that she had worn in her interview before she changed into the 'secretary' outfit with long black skirt white blouse and pumps.

She grinned. 'I'll do a lot of leg crossing. He won't know where to look.'

'And will you come for any legitimate reason?' Cherry asked me pointedly.

'We need to know where we stand with Ackroyd being dead. Does the deal look more attractive? We know already Randall's instinctive reaction, but what is his view now that the dust has settled? And does anything supply him with a motive for murder? Palmer seems to think that I might be Randall's assassin. I suppose Palmer could be right about Randall, but got the wrong assassin. Worth thinking about.'

Anji shook her head disbelievingly and gave a wide smile. 'I had no idea,' she said 'that this job would turn out like this. So fascinating, so exciting, so thrilling even. And two dead bodies already. Wow!'

'Let's try not to make it three,' said Cherry.

'Norman,' I said, 'tomorrow, can you and Morag check out the position on the Ackroyds' premises? I can't remember seeing it on the balance sheet as an asset, so my guess is that Fiona Ackroyd is now the owner. Good to know for definite, though. There are payments on the profit-and-loss analysis for rent — could be another lot of money going indirectly to Ackroyd. He's beginning to seem like a greedy man.'

'What are you going to do about Palmer lining you up for Ackroyd's death?' Cherry said.

'Only one thing for it — we launch our own investigation.'

* * *

Anji approved of the decision to play Secret Squirrel and clapped her hands.

'First stop,' I said, 'is Nancy, the receptionist. Let's see what she can remember about the events before and after the fire alarm going off. We'll go to see Randall in the morning, and back to Ackroyds after that. We'll widen our net by meeting some of the other solicitors as well as the two partners, Baker and Samson.'

'Maybe, tomorrow,' Norman said, 'we should look at the accounts side by side, to make a comparison of the situation as it stands and then run some spreadsheets.' He grimaced. Norman would be first to admit that he wasn't computer literate. But spreadsheets could be useful — with new assumptions like cutting the admin staff, moving offices from Ackroyds to an enlarged Randalls, that sort of thing.

'Martin had some useful comments,' I said. 'Reckoned Randalls was like a sweatshop. What's your view, Cherry?'

'I'm certainly the first one to leave at the official closing time of five thirty. I'll stay on later tomorrow to get a better idea.'

'Martin also said that Ackroyds was past its prime. Probably wouldn't survive in the not-too-distant future. Merging with Randalls — or effectively being taken over by them — might be a good solution in the longer term.'

The main courses arrived.

And so did Arthur.

* * *

A chair — a sturdy one — magically appeared and another place set at the table. Arthur ordered a steak — very rare — and poured himself a glass of the Pomerol.

'I'm bored,' he said. 'And I thought I'd find you here.'

Thinking wasn't Arthur's strong suit. He got there in the end, and I always valued his contribution, but it took him a while. That was why he had to give up wrestling. It took him too long to execute the rehearsed moves and his opponents got hurt: pretty soon no one would fight against him. He had to rely on door steward — bouncer — jobs to earn his income.

He was built like an ox. Underneath, though, he was a teddy bear. We all loved him.

'What's up?' I asked.

'Lost my job at the nightclub,' he said. 'Wouldn't let some oik in because he was bare chested. How was I to know he was the manager's son? I'm at a bit of a loose end.'

'Perfect timing,' I said. 'We have a job for you. But first, let's eat.'

We started to dig in, eating slowly so that Arthur would be able to catch up. His steak arrived with real home-made mustard and a ramekin of Toddy's ketchup for his chips.

'So tell me about this job?' he said.

'It's a little complicated,' I said.

'Don't make me laugh,' he said. 'Things are always a bit complicated when you're involved.'

'Thanks for the vote of confidence.' I explained about the current job with Ackroyds and Randalls, the headache of Ackroyd's death and the result of being viewed by the police as the prime suspect.

'You're right,' Arthur said. 'It is a bit complicated, even for you. How do I fit in with this?'

'I'd like you to follow some of the people who work for Ackroyds, maybe Randalls, too. Get some background information — lifestyle, living beyond their means, what they do out of the office, who they meet up with — anyone shady — the sort of thing that would help us to build a picture of them. Would they be a candidate for fraud, or in the frame for Ackroyd's murder? As you might have assumed, you better do as much as you can from your van — you're a little hard to miss.'

He nodded. 'When do I start? Not that I've anything better to do.'

'We'll get you some names and addresses in the morning. Start after they leave work in the afternoon.'

'Okay. Just one more question,' he said.

'Yes?' I asked, dreading some problem.

'Are we having another bottle of Pomerol?'

CHAPTER THIRTEEN

The three of us arrived at Randalls at nine in the morning, Anji dressed to kill. Cherry went for a demure outfit of a long summery dress and gold strappy slingbacks, so as to present a contrast and deflect Randall's attention. I pitied him for our two-pronged attack. So much confusion.

The Aryan Randall, blond hair swept back off his forehead, showed us into a conference room with a black table capable of seating twelve. He was wearing a fitted grey suit with a thin chalk pinstripe. No tie. His blue eyes popped out on stalks when he saw Anji. He pulled a chair out for her. Cherry and I were irrelevant.

'And who do we have here?' he said, looking lecherously at Anji.

'Anji,' she said. 'Just Anji.'

'Coffee, tea, water, juice — what can I get you, my dear?'

'Most kind, Mr Randall,' she said.

'Please, call me Richard.'

'I'm sure we'd all like a coffee,' she said.

'Won't be one moment,' he said, heading for the door.

Cherry smiled at me. 'Like taking candy from a baby.'

Randall returned, sneaking a peek at Anji's long legs.

'Ackroyd's death means a re-evaluation of the firm's net worth,' I said. 'We'd like to talk through some scenarios.'

Coffee then magically appeared, carried in by a brunette in a knee-length skirt and white halter-neck vest.

'Let me pour,' said Richard. 'How do we all like it?'

'Like my women,' I said. 'Hot and sweet.'

'Black or white?' he asked.

'Yeah.'

Two men joshing together. What fun.

I continued while Tricky Dicky poured, him glancing a little too long at Anji's tank top. If he wasn't careful, he would be spilling the coffee all over the tabletop.

'We're checking it out,' Cherry said, 'but our assumption at the moment is that the property is owned by Fiona Ackroyd, not the firm. Do you want to include that in the deal? What would you do with it? Sell it or rent it out or keep it?'

'I see us keeping it,' he said. 'It's conveniently situated for a barrister.'

'Like the ones who make coffee?' asked Anji.

'How sweet, dear girl.' He smirked. 'They are *baristas*. These are barristers. Like the wig and gown and up before the beak.'

Anji resisted the urge to play dumb on 'beak'. Don't want to overplay the role.

'I see us keeping it,' he repeated. 'I'd do it up and use it as a showcase for clients. We'd move all the staff here, maybe move up to a bigger office in time, and have client meetings there. They're bound to be impressed. Of course, it will all depend on the price, but, in theory, we would keep it.'

'Not the same for the staff, though?' asked Cherry. 'There'll be synergies between the two firms. What proportion of the staff would you hang on to?'

'We like to be lean on admin staff. I doubt there would be many we would keep. In your calculations, assume they will all be made redundant. Collateral damage, as they say. The solicitors and legal execs we would retain and fit them in here.'

'I don't suppose that you and your staff would remember their movements yesterday about three p.m.?' I said, changing the subject.

'Is that the time Ackroyd died?'

'That was the time he was murdered,' I clarified.

'Murdered?'

'Poisoned with strychnine, probably in his glass of Madeira.'

'At least he died the way he lived, eh?' he said, not missing a beat. 'Did have that thing about afternoon wine and cake. Everybody knows about it. I was thinking about keeping the tradition but now you've said that about a poison perhaps not. Poisoning the clients is off the agenda. Could put some people off.'

What great banter.

He poured himself another coffee, checked Anji's cup, and placed the flask on the table for Cherry and I to help ourselves. 'I was here all afternoon, my PA can vouch for that,' he said, 'but I could check with reception about any comings and goings.'

'Please do,' said Cherry. 'Be good to eliminate you all from the inquiries. Avoid a potential complication.'

He gave a short nod at Cherry. I could see he wanted to turn his attention back on Anji.

'Progress,' I said. 'Or lack of it. Recent events complicate matters, but we hope to deliver our conclusions by the end of next week. We've already started interviewing the solicitors and will make an assessment of those who would want to leave any new arrangement. It's a takeover rather than a merger now; that changes things. It's a people business, after all. You buy the people and the clients come with them.'

'Nice coffee,' said Anji, smiling sweetly. 'Is it instant?'

Randall spluttered indignantly into his cup. 'Jamaican Blue Mountain,' he said. 'Freshly roasted and coarse ground, so as not to lose its distinct flavour. Only the best for you, my dear.'

What a creep! I wondered about building some buffer in the calculations for potential harassment charges.

'Well, I think we can wrap things up. Anji will be here supporting Ms Walker from time to time.'

'You're welcome anytime, my dear.'

'We'll keep you posted,' I said. 'Won't be much longer. Be good to tie up things before the end of the month.'

I shook his hand.

As soon as were outside, I wiped it against my trousers to get the oil slick off.

'I can see why they call him *Dick*,' said Anji.

'It's Dicky,' I said. 'Tricky Dicky. But I echo your sentiments.'

'I feel dirty,' said Anji. 'Like I need a shower. How does he get away with behaving that way?'

'He pays well. When that's the case, people turn a blind eye.' I turned to Cherry. 'OK, Walker. Are you willing to spend a couple more days here? Should be easy to value this firm. From what you've shown me of the accounts, it seems like a simple operation. Talk to a few of the staff to get info on the working conditions and how they feel, then we'll wrap this side up.'

'Not a moment too soon,' Cherry said.

CHAPTER FOURTEEN

'What a jerk,' said Anji as we were driving back to our offices for her to shower — she was very insistent about that — and change, and for me to buy a big box of chocolates all wrapped up in fancy paper and a ribbon.

'Can we get him?' she said. 'Do something to protect the female staff?'

'Can't think of anything legal,' I said, 'but I'll work on it.'

'You do that,' she said, bristling after the morning's encounter.

'How far are you prepared to go to get retribution for him?' I asked.

'At the moment, I'm up for anything.'

'I'll bear that in mind. I liked the barista joke, by the way,' I said. 'I couldn't believe he fell for it.'

She gave a bitter laugh. 'Like Cherry said, candy from a baby.'

Morag was sitting at her desk going through a pile of papers when we arrived.

'Any messages?' I asked.

'Not for you, but one for Anji: Would you ring Mr Randall. He left his private phone number.'

'Huh!' she said, climbing up the stairs to use the shower in the bathroom. 'Bloody Randall.'

By the time I was back from buying the chocolates, she was freshly showered and dressed conservatively, ready for Ackroyds.

The phone rang. Morag answered and looked at Anji. 'It's Mr Randall for you again,' she said.

'Better answer it,' I said. 'Who knows, it might be something we can work on. Turn something to our advantage.'

She rolled her eyes and took the phone. 'Richard,' she said, with a giggle. 'Dicky. What can I do for you?'

I couldn't hear what he said in reply, but from Anji's reaction it sounded like it was suggestive.

Anji listened for a while and then said, 'That would be lovely. I'll see you then.'

Anji looked at me and made a gesture of poking her fingers down her throat.

'It seems,' she said, 'that Tricky Dicky has an interesting proposition for me. A job perfect for me with a salary too good to refuse. I'm having dinner with him this evening to discuss it. Could be interesting. If I can keep the food down, that is.'

* * *

Nancy was manning reception while typing up some arcane piece of legal jargon. She was wearing a pink twinset and a faux amber necklace. I couldn't see anything below the desk, but I guessed it would be something plain. I handed her the box of chocolates. She unwrapped them and looked puzzled. 'What is this for?' she said.

'For being a good receptionist. Nobody knows much about reception duties and what is involved. Receptionists are always underestimated and unappreciated. This is just a small gesture for what you have done for us. Not minding us getting in your way at times.'

'Thank you,' she said, blushing.

'And on top of us, you've had the police to contend with. Did they ask a lot of questions?'

'Mostly about what I was doing before the fire alarm went off. Comings and goings, you know?'

'Were you able to tell them anything useful?' Anji asked.

'Just the usual. People popping out for a cigarette or getting their americanos and lattes.'

'Were you given any help when the fire alarm went off? Maybe Mr Baker or Mr Samson? Marshalling the troops, like? Keeping everyone calm?'

'Didn't see either of them. When the alarm went off, I set the answerphone and headed straight outside. Oh, I had to put my shoes on — they're a new pair I was breaking in — too uncomfortable to wear them all the time. So I had my head under the desk for a little while. There were a few people outside already, but I couldn't vouch for anyone — it was a bit chaotic, to tell the truth. Hate to think what might have happened if it had been a real fire.'

'When were you aware that Roger Ackroyd hadn't come out of the building?' I asked.

'Only when you went back inside. I didn't know what you were doing. Thought you were being a bit foolhardy, probably about to grab some papers. Seemed like a daft thing to do.'

'Will you miss him? Roger?'

'He was a true gentleman. Born to a different age. A legal dinosaur. But he treated us well. Was always kind and caring. It's the end of an era.'

'Thanks, Nancy. I'm sorry about your loss. We'll get out of your hair. If you think of anything else, do let me know. Oh, and one more thing.'

'Which is?'

'Save me the Turkish delight.'

* * *

Everyone seemed busy that morning, perhaps working through Ackroyd's backload, keeping the wheels of industry turning. We fixed to see Baker at twelve and Samson in the afternoon. Meanwhile, we did secure some time with Carlton Seymour, one of the firm's solicitors. Not a partner. Be interesting to know what he thought about the current and future position.

Seymour was the right side of thirty and six-foot tall. I put him down as a gym fiend because the muscles of his upper arms seemed to stretch tight against the material of his suit jacket. He was black with short curly hair and tribal scars on both cheeks. He cut an imposing figure. A lawyer who would stand out in a crowd. He stood to his full height to welcome us, shook our hands and beckoned us to sit down on the opposite side of his desk. There were framed cuttings of past successes on the wall behind his seat, so a visitor could not miss them.

'How can I help you?' he said.

'We're novices in the legal world. Can you give us a summary of the type of business you handle?'

'As you must know, Ackroyds is a generalist rather than a specialist firm. Each of the solicitors handle a range of work — conveyancing, wills, power of attorney, corporate and so on. If one person is busy, the rest of us pitch in, just like the happy family we are. This is most often the case with conveyancing. People like to move on a Friday — it gives them the weekend to sort themselves out. The last Friday in the month is even worse — clients choose that day so their salaries or wages hit their bank account and they have a buffer before costs come in. The last Friday in the month is organized chaos. We all get involved and heave a sigh of relief when the weekend arrives.'

'What's the process in conveyancing? How does the system work?' I asked.

'Preparatory work starts at the first client meeting. In most cases, there then has to be the application for a mortgage. Once that is done, and any problems in the chain get cleared up, then we have to raise a deposit and exchange contracts — agree what will be the final legal terms on the deal.

Once contracts are exchanged, any last wrinkles are ironed out and we arrange completion. Money comes through from the mortgage lender or from the sale of the property and almost immediately goes to the seller's solicitor and on to the seller. And so it goes to all properties in the chain. If any element of any deal is delayed, the effects move down the chain. You're talking about minutes to complete the legal work. Thus, the chaos.'

'The money goes through the client account, is that right?' Anji asked.

We'd reconciled the client account transactions, so we knew that was the case. Good to get it confirmed, though.

'Correct,' said Seymour.

'And the next questions, Anji?'

'Who is authorized for transactions through the client account?'

'We all are,' Seymour said. 'All the solicitors and part-ners, that is. Transactions need to be authorized by Sarah Jenkins or Roger.' He paused. 'I know what you're thinking — too much opportunity for fraud — but we all need access to the client account to do our job. That's one of the draw-backs of being generalists. And if you can't trust a solicitor, who can you trust?'

'Was that Roger's thinking, too?' I said. 'What was he like to work for?'

'Benevolent dictator. We knew his quirks and suffered them — the afternoon ritual, for instance. Used to ask some of us to join him. Didn't like drinking alone. Perhaps he was too close to being an alcoholic. But he was good to me. Let me do some pro bono work.' He pointed to the frames on the wall. 'Not all firms are like that — most want to see money coming in all the time. I took in clients from the BAME community who could not pay for legal services — maybe some discrimination at work, harassment by the police . . . all worthwhile causes.'

'Talking of the police, how did you get on with Palmer? Seemed a strange chap to me.'

'A bit OCD, I would have thought. He moved a few of my files around into a neat pile before he sat down. Usual questions. What was I doing when the fire alarm went off. Told him I'd been busy, so didn't move at first. Thought it was a false alarm. It was only when I saw everyone else leave that I thought I should join them.'

'Most people's reaction, I would have thought,' Anji said.

'Presumably most of the staff were already outside when you left?' I said.

'Would they have seen me? Can they vouch for me, is that what you're thinking? Of course. I stick out like a sore thumb. Token black.' He went on: 'Then Palmer asked, when I had last seen Roger? I said, sometime before lunch, in person. But I saw Beryl with the tray about three.'

'Was that all?' I said.

'He asked about you. I don't think he likes you.'

'Common view, until you get to know me.'

'Then it gets worse,' said Anji with a sly grin.

'Back to business,' I said, shooting her a mock glare. 'Can you tell me how much business you handle?'

'I'd have to come back to you on that. We don't keep time sheets or such. I could look in my diary at the last month. That would refresh my memory, and we could go from there.'

'That would be good,' I said. 'Thanks for your time.'

We shook hands, and Anji and I went to the door.

'One more thing,' I said, 'Thinking about camaraderie, does the firm organize any social events?'

'No, we all keep ourselves to ourselves outside work.'

'What do you like doing when you're relaxing?'

'Listening to reggae with a glass of rum over ice in my hand. Mellow!'

* * *

'What did we learn from that?' Anji asked when we back in our office.

'Sloppy systems. Fraudsters' dream world.'

'And about him?'

'Not a team player. He said it. Sticks out like a sore thumb. Suffers it here because he can help people or causes with pro bono work. Can't imagine Randall being that tolerant.'

'What now?' asked Anji.

'Baker, then the person with the most control.'

'I thought you had him down as the one in control?'

'No, it's Sarah Jenkins. No one can do anything without her authorization.'

When we got to Baker's office the door was shut. We knocked and waited. No response. We knocked again and then just walked straight in. He was sat at his desk surrounded by a rain forest of paper.

'Ah, Shannon,' he said. 'Bad time. Working to a deadline. Can't see you now. Tell you what. Let me buy you lunch.'

Was this why the entertaining costs were abnormally high?

CHAPTER FIFTEEN

'Choose any sandwich you like,' Baker said.

Hey, big spender. We were sat at a rickety table in a pub specializing in real ale. This was a drinkers' pub. Its walls were yellow stained from nicotine over the years, the atmosphere was dark and depressing. Only the spit and sawdust were missing. For some reason, it was crowded. We took a table in the back where hopefully we could get some peace from the drinkers lining the bar. The only plus point was that red wine seemed to be on special offer; it had to be cheap to make up for all the negatives. It didn't look promising for our sandwiches.

Baker ordered a bottle of the house red, a surprisingly good Shiraz, took a sip and sighed. Must have been a hell of a tough morning.

'From what I heard at the bar, Ackroyd is the only topic of conversation,' he said. 'Any further news from the police?'

'If there was,' I said, 'I would be the last one to be told. Not on Palmer's Christmas card list. He seems to regard me as the prime suspect, and a particularly annoying one, too.'

'Strange that,' said Anji.

The sandwiches arrived. Huge slabs of white bread with ham and mustard for me, cheese and pickle for Anji. Baker passed. The only reason for the sandwiches for us was to soak up the alcohol.

'I'm tempted to ask how busy you are,' I said, 'but the answer seems to be self-evident.'

'Overworked and underpaid,' he said. 'Maybe that will change in the future.'

'And what will that future be?'

'It could be a cosy place. The staff are friendly — everyone gets on. With Ackroyd gone, we could make a tidy sum. He'd bled the place dry.'

'So, going solo or in with Randalls?'

'I'd vote to stay — as long as I'm senior partner. Reckon I'm the most qualified and running this place would be a doddle. Hate to be passed over.'

'I wouldn't think you'll stand any competition from Samson. Odd cove. What's it with the unusual glasses?'

'Eyes sensitive to light, apparently. Don't know the details.' He shrugged. 'But Randalls or stay? In reality, it would be Fiona's decision. Be a breath of fresh air either way. I joined here from my own business for security. I could get that either way, although from what I hear of Randall he'd squeeze every last drop of sweat from me. Small fish in a bigger pool. I hear he pays well, which would be a change.'

'As a partner, you'd be privy to the accounts. When we get back, can you break down the revenue between the legal staff? Percentage profit would be good, too. A rough guide will be fine. Not forgetting yourself, of course.'

'Of course,' he said. 'I could have a pretty good stab at that.'

The sandwich was beginning to cloy in my mouth. I noticed Anji was taking little nibbles of hers. I feigned not being hungry and pushed the plate away. Baker filled up his glass with more red wine. Seemed like he was in for a session.

'So, how's it going?' he said. 'Will it take much longer? Be good if you could wrap it up quickly.'

'We need a chat with both Sarah Jenkins and Fiona Ackroyd, but then it will be crunching the numbers. Out of interest, were you immersed in work when the fire alarm went off?'

'Crafty, Shannon.' He gave me a wry smile. 'You're playing private detective. Seeing if I have an alibi. Best leave that to the police. I can admit it to you, but no one else knows, I was out in the street having a secret smoke. No one knows about my disgusting habit.'

'Then no one can vouch for you?'

'Guilty as charged,' he said, leaning back in his chair and raising his hands in mock surrender. 'But what motive could I have for murdering Roger? I liked the old buffer, for all his faults. If you had a problem, whether business or personal, you could go to him and talk it through — everyone's favourite uncle — and then he'd help sort it.'

Satisfied I'd got everything I could from him — and couldn't wait to get away from the sandwich — I looked at my watch. 'Goodness, is that the time? Must dash. Thanks for the lunch.'

We shook his hand and pushed our way through the throng into some fresh air.

'No alibi,' said Anji.

'Hmm.' I nodded. 'Hard to be a secret smoker. The smoke clings to your clothes. In the circumstances, I doubt we'd get very far if we asked people whether he smelt smoky or not. Who's going to notice when the fire alarm is blaring out?'

'So, what next?' she asked.

'Take a look at the expense claims and book some time with Sarah Jenkins and Fiona Ackroyd. That will only leave Samson. My gut tells me that the solicitors will be a dead end and it's the two partners that will be of interest, but we'll still try them as a last resort. But first . . .'

'Yes?' said Anji.

'Let's pick up a decent sandwich.'

CHAPTER SIXTEEN

We ate our sandwiches sitting on a bench in the sun in Temple cloisters. It was a peaceful setting, far away from the clamour of the pub. At times barristers would walk past, some still begowned and some a little unsteady.

I set Anji the task of being paparazzo. Under the excuse of looking at offices needed now that Ackroyd was no more — was the same amount of space necessary and who will win the prize of his old office? — I wanted her to take pictures of the staff in situ. We needed something to show Arthur what our main targets looked like. While she was doing so, I went to see Sarah Jenkins.

She was wearing a beige top today, teamed with a plain silver necklace, no adornment. She could have been a chameleon lost against the honey emulsion of the walls of her office.

'Time to reconcile petty cash,' I said.

'Surely that isn't a consideration? Like it says, it's petty.'

'Got to tick all the boxes,' I said, feigning helplessness.

'Very well,' she replied with a huff.

Shannon strikes again.

She went to the filing cabinet, took out a bulging file and thumped it on the desk. 'There you go,' she said. 'All up to date to the end of the last month.'

Anji poked her head round the door. 'Smile,' she said and snapped a photo.

'What the hell was that for?' Jenkins said.

'Analysis of office space.' It seemed a bit lame, so I added, 'Plus snapshots of the key personnel. You're certainly one of the key personnel — run this function like a military campaign. Ackroyds would be lost without you. Randalls will value you.'

'Do you really think so?' she said, clearly appeased.

'No doubt.' I picked up the file and smiled, hoping to have made up lost ground. 'How does tomorrow afternoon sound for a longer chat?' I said. 'Say an hour at three?'

'OK,' she said, somewhat begrudgingly.

Good to generate enthusiasm.

* * *

'What did we learn from Baker,' Anji asked when we were back in our temporary office, 'apart from never to go to that pub again?'

'Got a drink problem. Unhealthy lifestyle. Wants security, which he would get at Randalls, as long as he kept bringing in the business and worked like a slave. Wants to be king bee, which he won't. Too conflicted.'

'So, in the end, it will be Fiona Ackroyd's decision as to whom she sells?'

'Which is why we're seeing her tomorrow.'

'Do you really think she would murder her husband?'

'I doubt it,' I said. 'But women murderers do have a penchant for poison — just take a look at Dorothy L Sayers's novels. But what about Baker? Is he the worm that turns? Gets revenge for being taken advantage of by Ackroyd?'

'He doesn't have an alibi,' Anji said. 'Can't rule him out.'

'We'll have Arthur follow him first. He seems to have most to gain from Roger's death if things go ahead according to his plan.' I sighed. 'Can we put off the tedious tasks before us?'

'Would be nice to,' Anji said, 'but nice isn't always the right solution, if my boyfriends are anything to go by.'

I explained that I wanted her to construct a spreadsheet to see who had claimed what, and what it was spent on. Meanwhile, I would start on the profit-and-loss valuation as to the point of Ackroyd's death and then forecast some scenarios from that point forward. They were centred around what revenue would be lost, what costs would be saved by cutting out Ackroyd's salary and partner share, and which staff needed to be culled. Not an enviable task. Beryl would be first in the firing line.

* * *

Meanwhile, I was intrigued by all the fuss about conveyancing and wanted to get a second opinion. Where better than Randalls? Kill two birds with one stone. I sent Anji home to get ready for her date and headed off. The rush hour was in full swing. I caught a cab which hardly moved, so I got out halfway and walked the rest.

Randalls' conveyancing specialist was Mandy Taylor, a well-preserved woman in her forties with black hair in a spiky pixie cut with a hint of grey at the roots. Her make-up was immaculate and sported a lipstick in blood red. She was modern for her age, blending in with the other females in the office, wearing a light-blue collarless top and a black skirt cut to just above the knees and black shoes with three-inch heels. She smiled at me and Cherry when we entered her office, which made a nice change. I liked her instantly. Her office walls were unadorned apart from a giant poster of the dramatic rock cliffs of St Lucia in the Caribbean. This was a woman with taste.

'I've already spoken to Ms Walker,' she said as we sat down opposite her. 'I don't know if I can add anymore.'

'I'm trying to get things in perspective,' I said. 'I've looked at conveyancing at Ackroyds and want to see how you operate, and whether there isn't a better way. But first, a little background, just to get some context. Tell me about yourself, Ms Taylor.'

'Call me Mandy,' she said. 'It's all first-name terms here, although there are times when I wish it wasn't — hard to get respect from the younger girls. So, where do I start?'

'They always say at the beginning,' I said, 'although that isn't always best, I find. Sometimes it's better to start with the end result and work your way back to causes. Thus, how did you get here?'

'Hard work and determination,' she said, 'but I doubt whether that is what you meant. But I'm being a bad host. Would you like coffee? Although it won't be up with Richard's Blue Mountain. His PA guards that with her life.'

'Coffee would be great,' I said.

Cherry said yes, too, and Mandy went off to get some. She came back along with a young girl in her teens carrying a tray. All part of the thrilling learning experience for an office junior. We took a mug each and sat back to relax. A rare event, it seemed, at Randalls.

'My story,' Mandy said. 'Grammar school, first from Cambridge in law. Spent five years at a small solicitor's practice specializing in conveyancing, moved up to a partnership in another law firm which was acquired by Randalls five years ago.'

'How does your home life function with the long hours you have to put in here?' I asked.

'My husband's a teacher at a grammar school, maths and business studies. Badly paid, but lots of long holidays. No children, so we can take advantage of the holidays and travel the world. Aims and ambitions? Make my mint, put lots in a private pension fund and retire early. Should be able to do that by the age of fifty-five, if all goes to plan.'

'Someone said to me that Randalls is long hours and high pressure: a cog in something turning. Is that how you feel?'

'I'm an easy-going sort of person,' she said. 'I get on with my work and take my money every month. Some people here take it too seriously, mindful of the target and the bonuses you get if you hit them. Stress is how you handle life — you create it yourself. I do yoga first thing in the morning. That calms me down, ready for whatever the day brings.'

'How might the takeover of Ackroyds affect you?' Cherry asked. 'Good or bad?'

'Neutral, I expect,' Mandy said. 'We're buying the people and the client list. Whatever conveyancing work comes, presumably the solicitor comes with it. Twice the work and twice the people to handle it.'

'Does everyone here feel that way?' I asked.

'I doubt it. There will be those who feel threatened by the arrival of new staff — more competition for bonuses and partner dividends. I think they're not the ones to worry. It's the staff at Ackroyds who should be the ones to be fearful. There'll be rationalization, jobs going in other words. Measured growth. It would be bad for the atmosphere if anyone from here goes. What's the business model if growth means job cuts?'

'What do you know about how Ackroyds handle conveyancing?'

'That they are in the dark ages,' Mandy said. 'Our system will terrify them. That's why we handle so much work here — the computer takes the strain. You prepare so much at the start — input the clients' details when the first instruction is received. The completion is then easy: one click and you're done.'

'What about Fridays and the last Friday in the month?' I queried. 'How do you cope with that?'

'It's the same. You prepare everything in advance. OK, it's busier, but as long as you work hard and stay calm, you can cope.' She paused and looked at me. 'You haven't asked the question you came to do.'

'And that is?'

'What was I doing at three p.m. when Ackroyd was killed,' Mandy said, holding my gaze.

'So what's your answer?'

'Here, working like a hamster running inside the wheel. But I imagine someone must have noticed if anything was amiss with the rest of the staff here. You could check at reception to see if there were any comings and goings. There must have been some client meetings, or people claiming they were at client meetings.'

'We started off thinking it was an inside job,' Cherry said, 'but soon realized anyone from outside could have done it if they could pick a lock. That includes people here.'

'And what do the police think?' Mandy said.

'That it was me,' I said.

'Bad luck,' she said, finding it hard to suppress the laugh. 'I can see where you are coming from now. They must be thrilled to have your input.'

'Rearrange the words *chickens* and *headless*,' I said.

'Nice one,' Mandy said. 'Well, they certainly haven't spoken to anyone here.'

'Exactly my point,' I said.

'So, you're playing amateur detective? What have you learned from me?'

'That you're not the type to commit a murder. Too calm, for one thing. Would have rationalized it as pointless. If what you say is true, you don't have money problems as a two-person-earning household.'

'All in all,' Cherry continued, 'you don't have a motive — money or love are the top two. You don't seem to have a grudge around Ackroyd, or to be fearful of the takeover. What would be the benefit of killing him?'

'Well,' she said with a smile, 'I can rest easy tonight, without wondering when the police are going to come and break the door down.'

I guessed from her tone that it was time to call it a day. We'd learned all we could. We left Randalls and the number of staff still slaving over hot computers at half six in the evening. We got a taxi back to Ackroyds, picked up the Beamer and joined the exodus from London. Crawled home in comfort.

CHAPTER SEVENTEEN

'Wow!' said Cherry as Anji walked into our second-floor room where we were all gathered.

'Blimey!' said Arthur.

Anji had showered and changed for her dinner with Randall. She was hoping it was an appointment; he that it was a date. She was wearing a (very) little black dress and killer heels with lots of straps. Her long blonde hair was loose and curled and hung past her shoulders and gleamed in the light of the room.

'Wow!' Cherry said again. 'Randall doesn't stand a chance.'

Anji smirked.

The doorbell rang, signalling that the cab he had ordered had arrived.

'Any last minute instructions for me?' Anji asked.

'If he offers you a job, take it as long as you can start the day after tomorrow. It would be good to have a spy in the camp.'

'Right. Wish me luck,' she said as she went down the stairs.

I looked across at Arthur. 'Don't let her out of your sight.'

* * *

Morag, clad in her clan McClennan kilt skirt and a white frilly blouse to show allegiance with Scotland, got us soft drinks. We were still on duty. No one was allowed alcohol until Anji was safely back. The four of us sat down and placed our papers on one of the coffee tables.

'Ratios,' Norman said. 'What's your feeling?'

The price for a company under sale is often based on a ratio of profit after tax. The higher the ratio, the greater the price. Conversely, the lower the ratio, the lower the price. It wasn't all about that; any properties or valued fixed assets had to be taken into account too. That wasn't going to be the case for Ackroyds, as there were no fixed assets or property — that would be subject to a separate negotiation with Fiona Ackroyd.

'Ackroyds first, Nick,' said Norman.

'As it stands today, it's basically nothing. It's not made a profit for the last three years. Ackroyd bled it dry. With him gone, then all his basic salary and add-ons can be put straight in profit, although there might be some revenue drop if his clients move their business or die off. Then you have to look to the future. Streamlining the business, you could cut staff and the wage bill — that's where synergy comes in. Randalls would be profiting by synergy. He's basically buying the solicitors and their clients. I need to talk to all of them to get a realistic feel of what will follow them to Randalls.'

'And at the end of the day?' Norman asked.

'No more than five times. It's going to take a lot of work to pull it off. My calculations at this point would be five times a best-case profit of a hundred and fifty grand — seven hundred and fifty thousand — with Ackroyd gone, and then it's something like one point five million with synergy.'

'How about Randalls, Cherry? What's your best guess?

'Profitable company, well managed, very streamlined, good long-term plan. All in all, very attractive. I would reckon a ratio of eight.'

'So Randall buys at a ratio of five,' Norman said, 'and the value of his company rises at a ratio of eight. Buy at one and a half million, value at eight times that which is an added value of three times one and a half million — four and a half million. You can see why they call him Tricky Dicky.'

'And, of course, he won't want to pay that much,' said Cherry. 'The shares aren't of much use to Fiona, and Baker and Samson hold ten per cent each. No one is going to play hardball. Lick your lips and rub your hands.'

'And Fiona still has the money to come from selling the property,' said Norman. 'I'll get in touch with some high-end agents tomorrow and see what they think it might make.'

'So where do we go from here?' said Cherry.

'I need to talk in more detail to Samson and to the other solicitors, which will take a few days, and I want to interview one more solicitor at Randalls.'

'Who?' Cherry asked.

'Whoever handles criminal work,' I said. 'I've been thinking about Palmer's theory that I could be Randall's assassin. It's not a bad idea, apart from the part about it being me. Whoever handles the criminal cases could have friends in low places, who might do the deed for money or as a favour.'

'Okay,' said Morag slowly, trying to keep track of my movements. 'And from there?'

'I want to be there on Friday to see how the system for conveyancing works in practice. Wrap it all up by the last Friday of the month.'

I crossed the room to the big window, looked down at the street below and checked my watch.

'I want to talk about Anji before she gets back,' I said. 'She's done everything we asked of her with no questions. She's seen two dead bodies and not flinched. She's having dinner with an obvious predator. She knows when to ask questions and when to be silent. She's becoming invaluable. With more experience, she will be a big asset. She's on a small salary of two grand a month while we had a good look at her. I want to put that up to three. Any thoughts?'

'Do it,' said Cherry.

'You know I like to watch the costs,' said Norman. 'But in this case, she's worth it.'

'What about you, Morag? You deserve a vote, too. We couldn't do without you, either. You're just as much a part of the team'

Morag nodded. 'I agree. She's one in a million. Go for it.'

I checked my watch again. She should be here by now. I heard the toot of a horn — the tinny sound that the one on Arthur's van made. They were back.

The taxi pulled up and Anji and Randall got out. He kissed her on the cheek while his hand touched her on the bottom. She broke the clinch and waved as she stepped through the door. A moment later she joined us, Arthur close behind.

'Has you been watching me all this time?' she asked.

'Every minute,' he replied.

'Well,' I said, 'come and sit down and tell us all about it.'

She sat down and took off her shoes. 'They've been killing me,' she said, rubbing her feet. 'It was a swanky restaurant — nowhere near as good as Toddy's — full of businessmen and their mistresses. Low lighting, lots of pink tablecloths and napkins. Randall had ordered champagne and it was there in an ice bucket ready to serve, the waiter poured and Randall gave a cheesy cheers to me. What for, I don't know, but that would become clearer as the evening progressed.' She glanced around. 'Can I have a drink? I've been pacing myself all evening.'

Morag went to the fridge and took out a bottle of champagne, expertly opened it, poured her a glass and looked at the rest of us. We nodded and she poured more glasses.

'He was wearing a beige suit and black shirt,' Anji continued. 'Randall looked like he could have come straight from work or the mafia monthly meeting. We ordered — there were those menus for women with no prices. Keeping in character, I had a posh version of prawn cocktail as a starter — far too fancy if you ask me — and their take on fish and chips for the main.' She sipped her champagne. 'He couldn't keep his eyes off me. I even made what I reckoned was an unnecessary trip to the loo so he could take another look at my legs where the dress had risen up. It was barely decent.'

'Was there any conversation while this was going on?' I asked, 'or had you robbed him of the ability to speak?'

'He wanted to know what I did after I left work — told him Pilates and described the tight Lycra I wore for it. He was slavering.' She laughed. 'I had to tell him about my weekends and whether I went anywhere with my boyfriend — told him I was between boyfriends. Next was all about my work here — what were my duties — I made it sound boring. He said I would fit in well with him. I was ideally suited. And all this time he was touching my hand.'

'And so?' Cherry asked. 'What was the outcome of all this?'

'I am now a fully-fledged administration executive, starting tomorrow, at a salary of thirty thousand a year.'

'Excellent. Now for stage two,' I said. 'Morag, will you go down to Tottenham Court Road — there's lots of places selling electronic gadgets there — and buy what the spooks call a wire. We want something discreet that Anji can wear at work so we know what's happening.' I raised my glass. 'Let's have a toast, we have a reason for a celebration. Anji, your probationary period is now over. We all agree that you are priceless. We're giving you a fifty per cent increase in salary.'

'Fifteen per cent.' She grinned. 'That's marvellous.'

'Not fifteen per cent,' Cherry said. '*Fifty* per cent. And the flat thrown in free. Congratulations.'

Anji was speechless for a moment, staring at us. 'I don't know what to say, but thank you all. Frankly, I'd work here for fifty per cent less.'

'You're welcome. Now,' Norman took us down to earth, 'why are we doing this?'

'Because men like Randall shouldn't be able to prey on young women,' Cherry said. 'He needs to be taught a lesson.'

'And,' said Anji, 'because it's fun.' It was then that we heard a noise — a thump in the office downstairs. Burglars, was my first thought. I rushed downstairs. Empty. I opened the front door and saw someone outside. It was a youth with a hood draped across his face. He was in the act of picking up a brick to have another go at smashing the window but I knew he'd need an atomic bomb to get past the specially strengthened glass and the loose wire coating; it was designed to bounce back a Molotov cocktail.

He saw me and started to run. I set off after him. We ran along the old streets and alleyways of Docklands, me gaining all the time.

He was out of shape — should have had the regime of running about Island Gardens that I had with Arthur — it was inevitable that I would get him. He skidded to a halt in one of the alleys and turned to face me. He pulled a knife, big one, long blade.

I kept my distance.

In normal situations, I would have had on some sort of coat that I could have wrapped around my left arm as a protective shield against the knife. but who wears a coat indoors?

He pointed the knife at me. 'Don't come any further,' he said, 'or I'll stick you.'

'Whoa,' I said. 'It doesn't need to be like this. No harm done. Drop the knife and walk away.'

I edged forward. Arthur used to tell me that if you can't win clean, then go dirty. I edged another foot closer, preparing for the latter.

'Stay where you are,' he shouted, waving the knife.

'Easy,' I said. 'You've got me covered. I can't do you any harm.'

The knife was shaking in his grasp. I guessed he hadn't used it before, an experienced knife bearer would have stabbed away and run like the hounds of hell were after him. Didn't make him less deadly, though. Made him unpredictable, and that's dangerous in itself.

'In a moment,' I said, 'a six-foot-five man will come along and pick you up like a twig, bend you backwards so that your head will be looking at the view behind you. But before that . . . why did you do this?'

I edged further forward again.

'Some bloke in the pub,' he said, his voice shaky, 'must have seen me and my friends and heard us bragging about what we had done. Reckoned us up for anything that made a fast buck. Said all he wanted me to do was to throw a brick through a window — he even gave me the brick with a note on it. A hundred pounds up front, and another hundred when I'd done the job. Seemed like easy money.'

He walked towards me. I let him get closer and, at the right time, kicked him in his balls. He dropped the knife and fell to his knees, clutching his testicles and writhing in pain. I kicked the knife into the gutter.

'Tell me about this man,' I said, giving him another kick in the testicles (remember, fight dirty), though softer this time.

'What did he look like?' I said.

'Just a bloke, you know?' he gasped. 'Nothing special.'

'White or black?' I said.

'White.'

'How old?'

'Couldn't tell,' he said.

'Try harder.' I gave him another nudge.

'Look, if I tell you about him, I could make it to his hit list. Nobody likes a stool pigeon. Lose my mates, too.'

'The other way is that you lose any ability to have children,' I said. I gave another nudge, harder this time.

He doubled up in pain.

'How old,' I repeated.

Then the equation changed. Three youths came to join us.

'Having a spot of bother, Wayne?'

They circled me. Knives came out.

'Let's get this over and done with,' one of them said.

'Yes, let's,' said another voice. And Arthur emerged from the shadows. He threw a towel in my direction. I wrapped it around my left arm and saw that Arthur had done the same. We could have been boy scouts. Always be prepared.

'Who's first in line?' Arthur said.

A youth leapt towards him. Arthur swatted him like a fly with a back handed slap to the face. I advanced on one of the others. There was no fight left in Wayne, so he just lay there, taking in the fun.

My opponent couldn't have been much more than seventeen. He had gone before I ever got near to him. The last of the four made a passable effort not to run, but I simply brushed aside the knife and I hit him with a straight left to the head. He reeled backward, and I hit him in the solar plexus, twice. He doubled up and fell to the ground.

Arthur had his foot on the chest of his assailant. 'Now what was it you needed to know, Nick?'

'Tell me about the man who hired you,' I said to our two prisoners. 'What did he look like?'

'He was old, man, you know?' Wayne said.

Which was helpful, seeing that old was anyone over the age of twenty.

'Hair colour?' I persisted.

'Sort of brown. Old-fashioned style.'

Which probably meant anyone that was not shaved at the sides.

'He was wearing a camouflage jacket, trying to look cool. But he still looked like a victim. Thought we could get some money out of him. Just a bloke,' Wayne said. 'We don't know any more.'

Arthur kicked his man and then spread his hand out. He put his boot on the youth's fingers and stamped. There was the sound of bones cracking.

'Get out of here,' Arthur said.

They headed for the hills, Wayne being half-carried by his friend.

'Any point going back to the pub for when the guy comes back?' I said.

'What do you think?' he said.

'Snowflake in hell,' I said.

'Yep.'

CHAPTER EIGHTEEN

Fiona Ackroyd had phoned the previous day asking for a meeting at her house — it wasn't *their* house anymore — at nine a.m. The Ackroyd residence was a Victorian four-storey house in Dulwich Village, one of the most sought-after areas close to the centre of London. Why they needed such a big property — presumably, given their ages, the children had left the nest — was a puzzle, but people were not always rational about their choice of home. For example, would anyone have bought our Docklands property as a home?

Fiona met Anji and me at a stained-glass porch and beckoned us with a smile. Not many people had the same attitude when it came to our visits. A good start. She was wearing a long floral dress and pink slippers that did more for practicality than stylish appearance. She took us through to the lounge where a stainless-steel flask of coffee had been laid out with cream and sugar. The room, though large, was not really big enough to accommodate the three wide sofas set around a working fireplace. The sofas bore the depressions of a long life and were bamboo-patterned which complemented the pale green walls. It all seemed a bit old-fashioned and would have benefitted from a bit of TLC.

Fiona poured the coffee, both Anji and I eschewing the cream.

'Good of you to take time to see us,' I said, as I sank into one of the sofas.

'I'd like everything sorted as soon as possible,' she said. 'Roger wasn't the best at managing finances, so I'm not sure where I stand. I've had offers already on the offices, generous ones from what I can tell, but I'll give Randall first refusal if he buys my shares. Keep everything as simple as possible.'

'What would you like to see happen to the practice?' I asked.

'I would like to see it carried on, for the staff's sake if nothing else, but I guess that is wishful thinking. Whether it's a management buyout or selling to Randall, the numbers would need to be drastically reduced. The world moves on. Sad, though.'

Sad indeed: nothing would be the same again.

'This is a nice house,' said Anji. 'Must be a big mortgage?'

'We settled the mortgage years ago,' Fiona said. 'We own it outright. That's one thing, at least, which is not a complication.'

'Tell me about the offices in Temple?' I said. 'Freehold or leasehold?'

'Leasehold with ninety-five years left. Someone could buy the freehold, but I imagine that would be a massive sum.'

'Did Roger ever mention a value on the business?'

'Roger hadn't thought of it as a business for many a year now. It was a plaything for him, a hobby. Should have retired years ago, but he would have been lost for something to do. Didn't play golf or have any interest in sport; played bridge badly; didn't collect stamps or any other diversion of that sort. His life was the practice. The practice was his life. And now it's all over.'

She took a handkerchief from the sleeve of her dress and dabbed at her eyes. I drank some of my coffee to give her time to recover. It was an arabica made in a cafetiere, my tastebuds told me, and decanted into the vacuum flask. I wished there had been a better opportunity to savour it.

After I moment, I decided it was safe to continue. 'Will this be a sale purely for the most money, or do you lean towards a deal that preserves the Ackroyds' heritage in some way?' I asked, dreading the answer. Beryl and her like were still on my mind.

'It's the money,' she said. 'Maximize the inheritance that will be left for our sons and our grandchildren.'

'Well, you can rely on us to get you a fair price,' Anji said, caught up in the moment, too. 'Nick has principles. Won't be swayed from the right thing to do. Don't worry. You can rely on him.'

I gave what I hoped was a reassuring nod. 'Was Roger insured at all?' I asked. 'Either private life insurance or through a key man policy paid for by the practice?'

'No, neither. Roger thought he was invincible.'

'Have the police been kind to you?' I asked, switching to the hidden agenda.

'I suppose they're just doing their job,' Fiona said. 'Professional, but without much caring. I couldn't help much. Knew nothing about poisons or who might want to kill him.'

'Did Roger have any enemies?'

'Not that I could think of. I'd rule out the staff, but it seems that may be where the murderer is lurking. If there were any outside the practice that held a grudge, how would they know of the teatime ritual? It's got to be an inside job. When I was there yesterday for the meeting, I found it hard to look at anyone without being suspicious.'

'What about Baker and Samson? They have the biggest motive.'

'Samson wouldn't hurt a fly. Too lily-livered for that. Lacks the courage. Needs a jolly good reason to do anything, let alone murder.'

'And Baker?' I asked.

'Now, he's different. Wants to be top dog but wouldn't take any action to make that happen. Goes along with the easy option. That's why he wouldn't be good at running the show. No drive.'

'We saw Carlton Seymour,' Anji asked. 'What's your opinion of him? Did he have designs on being a partner and was aggrieved that he wasn't given that promotion?'

'Carlton is a different kettle of fish. Always takes on the mantle of the underdog. Fighting injustice is all he cares about. He has no reason for murder. In fact, the sale or merger, whatever you like to call it, may limit his pro bono work in the future. Roger was very understanding about that.'

'Any others?' I asked.

'No one who would hold a grudge or would want to get revenge for something.'

'Did the police ask about your movements on the day?' I asked.

'Yes, but I don't think their heart was in it. If I wanted to poison him, I could have done that anytime at home. I had an alibi, too. WI meeting. Many who can vouch for me there, although there was a rather boring talk on Constable, so some of them may have dropped off.'

'Anything else that might be useful?' I asked. 'Any debts, addictions?'

'Nothing.'

'Thanks, Fiona. We'll get out of your hair now. Let you grieve in peace.'

Anji and I prised ourselves out of the depth of the sofas and shook her hand. Fiona showed us out and nodded as we drove away.

Mission accomplished, though no further ahead. Story of my life.

CHAPTER NINETEEN

'Interesting,' Anji said when we were back in the office at Ackroyds.

I looked up from what I was doing and saw her pause in the checking of the expenses. We were back to minutiae and had discounted Fiona Ackroyd from our suspects for either fraud or the larger crime of murder. She had nothing to gain by defrauding the practice. To have killed Roger, she would have had to hire an assassin or have an accomplice. All too complex.

'What's interesting?' I asked.

'These expenses. We have a creature of habit. This one has exactly the same meal at the same time. Same amount.'

'Let me see.'

'Here,' she said. 'Entertains a different client each week and the amount matches twice.'

It was evident what was going on, and a surprise that no one had spotted it before.

'A fiddle,' I said. 'At the end of the meal he is given a paper bill. He pays the bill by credit card and is given a receipt for that. He keeps the original paper bill and submits that another week. He's only entertaining a client, or who-ever it is that he entertains, once a fortnight in reality, rather than once a week. It's not a vast amount, a few hundred quid a month, but it is a fraud nonetheless. And who is this?'

'Baker,' she said.

* * *

Sarah Jenkins didn't get up when we entered her room. She hadn't ordered any tea or coffee and there were no biscuits on a plate. Quite a welcome.

'Tell me, Sarah,' I said, after we had put the thick petty cash file on her desk, 'how do you feel about the Randalls' prospect — sale, merger, takeover . . . whatever you like to call it?'

'The most likely Randalls' prospect for me is redundancy,' she said. 'Failing that, it would be fitting in with new systems and red tape, being swallowed up, essentially. I like it here. I'm effectively my own boss. No one interferes with what I do. They just let me get on with it. It's a good crowd, too. The office staff are friendly and the solicitors are not all high and mighty. It's an easy life. I'd miss it.'

'You get on well with the solicitors, all ten of them plus the partners? Any favourites?'

'Some of them are a bit disorganized, which sometimes makes life difficult, especially on a Friday when completions hit their peak, but I can't complain.'

'How about Baker? Do any favours for him?'

Her expression didn't change. 'I don't know what you mean.'

'Come on, Sarah. You're an intelligent woman. You must have spotted what he's been doing. Anji picked it up easily, and she's new to the business. Did you turn a blind eye or did he cut you in on it? A bit of extra cash in your back pocket?'

She sighed. 'A blind eye, I suppose. It was only a couple of hundred quid a month. Seemed so trivial. The practice could afford it. Wasn't going to make any difference.'

'And you didn't speak to Baker about it? Warn him off?'

'I didn't feel it was my job to question a partner. I just let it slip through. No harm done.'

Anji could hold her tongue no more. 'Was he aware you knew what was going on?' she asked. 'It could have backfired on you. A test of your honesty — and you failed.'

'I can't answer that. He never said anything. I see the risks now. What are you going to do?' Jenkins asked, her composure slipping.

'I don't know,' I said. 'Talk to Baker and give him the opportunity to pay back the money. That will at least tidy things up. As for your part in the fraud, I'll think about it. You do realize you've put us in a very invidious position? I'm not sure if I can overlook this without breaking our contract with Randalls or, indeed, Ackroyds.'

'I won't do anything like it again. I promise.'

'Anything else you would like to admit to? It would count in your favour if you save us the trouble putting in a lot of tedious work. We'll find out in the end.'

'No, nothing. I swear.'

'If you were in our shoes, who would be the most likely candidate for fraud?'

'I couldn't pick out anyone. Would have to be one of Mr Baker or Mr Samson or the solicitors, I suppose. No one else would have the opportunity. You might have to include Mr Ackroyd, too. He had the most power over the finances.'

I decided to switch tack. 'What can you remember about when the fire alarm went off?'

'I was adding up some figures when the alarm sounded. I didn't want to be interrupted, and, anyway, it's always a false alarm, isn't it? John Samson banged on my door and insisted I leave. By the time I was outside, there was already a large crowd. After that there was a lot of milling about — organized chaos, you might say.'

'Did you notice Roger Ackroyd was missing?'

'Not until you went back into the building. I thought that might be the only reason for such a dangerous move.'

'Does Roger's authority on the bank accounts still apply?'

'Yes. I haven't got round to deleting him.'

'I'd like the passwords, PIN, whatever is needed for him to make payments and transfers. I also want the same for your authority.'

'That's a big ask. You would be able to effectively control the whole banking system of the practice. Why should I trust you that much?'

'Because I have a loose mouth. I can get you sacked at a whim and I can report you to the police. Goodbye, future jobs — who wants a fraudster on the payroll? — as well as this one.'

'Okay,' she said hurriedly. 'I can arrange that. Anything else while you have me at my weakest?'

'Not at the moment. Just don't leave the country.'

Anji and I went back to our office. As soon as we were there, Anji started asking questions.

'Why did you let her off the hook?' she demanded.

'Because I now have her in my pocket. We can do whatever we want to safeguard the practice. Remember this. If a fraudster gets away with something once, he or she might think it worth trying again with a larger prize.'

'So what next?' she said.

'I think it's time for another chat with our Mr Baker. We have leverage.'

CHAPTER TWENTY

'You know, don't you?' said Baker when we made an unappointed visit to his office. 'I saw you talking to Sarah. You took a long time to work it out.'

'What do you know?' I said. 'Spill the beans.'

The next lesson for Anji: if you keep quiet, you may learn more.

'It was stupid of me,' he said. 'Sometimes you have to beat the system, otherwise you're just a cog in something turning.'

'I'm hearing that expression more and more. So you're saying the money wasn't important?' Anji asked, learning more from each new experience.

'It was just the thrill of it. I don't need the money. It was getting away with it. Not being a slave to the machine.'

'Do you think that Roger had any inkling of what you were doing?' I asked.

Baker shook his head. 'He didn't micromanage. Just as long as the money kept rolling in to pay his salary, with a bit left over for a dividend, he was happy.' He paused. Then looked pale. 'You're not suggesting that would be a motive for murdering him? I told you, I was nowhere near the office when the fire alarm went off.'

'Which no one can corroborate,' I said. 'Small beer, but plenty people have been killed for less. You did stand to lose your job if you were found out. And then the world caves in.'

'I don't think I want to answer any more questions.'

'I think you need to answer any questions we ask. We have power over you now. We can report you in our findings to Randall, and I can tell DI Palmer what you've done. What will they make of it? Probably be less understanding than us.'

He capitulated. 'What do you want from me?'

'First, I want you to repay the money. How long has this been going on?'

'A couple of years.'

'Two years?'

'Well, more like three, I suppose.'

'Let's say two hundred pounds for thirty-six months.'

'Seven thousand two hundred pounds,' said Anji.

He gulped.

'Soon mounts up, doesn't it? Fix it with Sarah,' I said. 'She's known all along, so you don't need to explain. Nice try with the sandwiches, by the way. Frugal. That's the impression you were trying to create.'

'What then? Am I off the hook?'

'It will count in your favour if we decide to say what you've been doing. We have a moral dilemma as well as a possible breach of contract to consider. No promises.'

* * *

As we were about to leave, Palmer arrived.

'Not so fast, Shannon. I have some more questions for you.'

'Didn't you hear Martin say he will charge you with harassment?'

'I could charge you with withholding information.'

'And what information would that be?' I asked.

'I don't know, because you're withholding it.'

Lord help us!

'How does this sound?' Palmer said. 'You have the drink and cake with Ackroyd, pouring strychnine unnoticed into his glass. You wait for him to die, pocket the glass, go out the back door in the way you showed me, locking it. You then dash inside to set off the fire alarm and then dash outside again to hide round the corner until a crowd starts to form and nobody knows what's going on. You then come out of hiding and lose yourself in that crowd.'

'How does it sound?' I fired back. 'Sounds like a Whitehall farce with all the comings and goings in and out of doors. Fanciful, at the very least. Desperate at the extreme. I will not be a patsy to your quest to retire on a high note rather than with a failure. And, inconveniently for you, Anji was with me all the time. Thus, I have an alibi.'

Anji nodded.

'You could have put pressure on her to alibi you. Threatened to sack her. Bribed her, maybe.'

'I know you don't like me, and I can understand that — I'm a smart arse who can rub people up the wrong way — but you would be better off looking for someone without an alibi. Baker, for example.'

'How do you know he didn't have an alibi?'

'Just came up in conversation.'

'Have you been meddling in police business?'

'Me, sir? No, sir; not me, sir.'

'You're doing it again, Nick,' Anji said.

'I know. Can't resist it.'

'You think you're so clever, Shannon,' Palmer said.

'It's all relative,' I said.

CHAPTER TWENTY-ONE

Anji went off to Randalls dressed in a short white skirt and a dark brown blouse with the top two buttons undone revealing just a hint of bra — no midriff-bare tank top today; we needed something that hid the wire.

When I arrived at Ackroyds, Palmer was nowhere in sight, so I went straight to Baker's office, took a letter Morag had typed up for me earlier that morning out of my briefcase and laid it on the table in front of him.

'I want you to sign this. You're retiring at the end of the month for health reasons. You'll take it to Samson, who will now be the senior partner, and get him to tell all the staff. Clear your office by Friday at the end of the next week and never come back. I'll cover up the fiddling of expenses as long as you pay back the money today.'

'Done it already,' he said, not meeting my eyes. 'Handed a cheque to Sarah earlier.'

'You'll find another job or go solo, and you'll have the money from the shares as a buffer while you get back on your feet. I'll cover it from Randall — make out it was an advance on the profit share because you had some financial difficulties. Tell him that Roger authorized it. Now, sign it.'

I slid him my fountain pen and he picked it up after staring down at it for a moment.

'I don't know whether to thank you or not,' he said.

'Do what you will,' I said, 'as long as you sign it.'

He scrawled something that was possibly a signature. Blew on it to dry the ink.

'Let's get this over and done with,' he said, getting up from his chair and walking to the door. 'Time to give Samson the good news — one less person in the profit share for next year, ours or Randall's.'

* * *

I let Samson absorb the import of Baker's retirement before calling in on him. I was still fixated by the tinted glasses and lack of eye contact. It made him mysterious.

'I suppose you're behind this, Shannon,' he said. 'Pretty Machiavellian, I would think. What am I meant to do now?'

'Take it on the chin and do what you have to. The Baker resignation causes a temporary problem. Pretend sympathy when you tell the staff. I expect they'll blame me, so you'll be off the hook.'

'What else do you want from me?'

'I need some background. Tell me precisely what you do here.'

'Conveyancing, mainly. It's our bread and butter. If that's slow, I help out on wills, powers of attorney and trust funds. Exciting stuff, hey?'

'You chose the career, not me.'

'Indeed. So I deserve all the sympathy I can get.'

'How long have you been here?' I asked.'

'Eleven years in all. Did my articles here after leaving university. It's an easy place to work — no pressure, nice staff. Got stuck in a rut, I suppose.'

'If you don't mind me saying so, or even if you do, you seem young to be a partner here.'

'I can be persuasive when I have to. I threatened to leave a couple of times. That did the trick, climbing higher up the greasy pole.'

'And what will you do when you have Randall as your boss? He won't be such a pushover.'

He shrugged. 'I hear he pays well. That's a good start.'

'And he wants his pound of flesh for it.'

'Well, I want to earn a pile and stash it. Give up on the weather in this country and retire somewhere hot and sunny, and all that by the time I am forty-five.'

'Randall will want you to stay late,' I persisted. 'How much will that affect your private life?'

'Might be more stimulating than what I have now. Safe marriage, pesky kids, all humdrum, nothing to hold me here.'

I noticed he didn't say *us*. Evidently his family wasn't part of his retirement plan.

'How wedded are your clients to you?' I asked. 'Will they transfer to Randalls?'

'The time lag on returning their business is about five years — that's the average time people move. Much of the work comes through recommendation. I've got a good reputation and there's no reason for those recommended not to transfer their business. They're buying me, basically.'

'Which puts you in a strong bargaining position.'

'I hope so,' he said. 'Does it look like the takeover will happen?'

'Different options, but some are looking good to date. I don't think Baker's retirement will hurt it too much, but I need to crunch another set of figures. Won't be long now.'

'If you'll excuse me,' he said, in a voice of finality, 'but I have things to do to keep the wheels in motion. Come back another time when I'm not so busy — especially not on Friday. Thank you.'

The verdict from all the staff seemed to be unanimous. The pay wasn't great, but it was a nice place to work. Left to your own devices, stress-free, and the staff were friendly. It was a big happy family. Unanimous, or pretty much so.

* * *

The dissenting voice belonged to a man in his early forties called Graham Kirby. He looked like an Open University professor in a shabby tweed jacket with leather patches on the elbows. At the bottom of his cord trousers, a pair of suede shoes peeked out — stained and should have been replaced if he wanted to blend into an Islington set or some militant faction of Labour in a cosy suburb. His long hair was unkempt.

'Kirby,' he said, gesturing at a set of two chairs set at the opposite side of a confused desktop. Here was a man lost in his work. 'Call me Graham. I like to encourage informality. Helps with my line of work.'

'Which is?' I asked.

'Predominantly family. Divorces, access to children, settlements, that kind of thing. You see the rotten side of life in those seats.'

'Is it profitable, to make up for the trauma it must cause?'

He swept the hair from his eyes. 'Barely. I suspect I might not make the cut with Randalls. It jogs along and can be emotionally rewarding. Roger was sympathetic to it. Reckoned it helped our image. Caring, you know?'

'What would it take for the Randalls' deal to be scuppered?' I asked.

'Rebellion. Rally the troops. Get Fiona Ackroyd on side. Persuade her to go for a management buyout. I'm not rich, but I could chip in something. Baker going complicates things — I don't suppose you had anything to do with that? — but he'd sell his shares if it came to it. Can't afford not to, now he's going.'

'And—'

'And,' he interrupted, 'I can't remember what happened when the fire alarm went off. Too much confusion and milling around. Can't alibi anybody, and, I suspect, no one can alibi me definitely.'

'What did Palmer make of that?'

'Frustration,' he said. 'Would have been a happy bunny if I'd seen someone go into Roger's office carrying a phial of strychnine and the word *killer* tattooed on his forehead. I heard Linda next door clapping her hands to rouse everyone, finished dictating a letter into the machine — it's always a false alarm, isn't it? — and joined the throng. It's disconcerting, must be an inside job — who else would have a motive for killing Roger? — so I don't know who to trust anymore.'

'Who are the bookies' favourites, do you think?'

'I'm not a stool pigeon, Shannon,' he said, leaning back in his chair, forcing more distance between us. 'Not for the police or for you. I'm not going to blacken anybody's character for no reason.'

'Worth a shot,' I said.

* * *

I retreated to the company of Beryl, hopefully a sane voice among the chatter.

'How's it going?' I asked.

'Baker leaving is a bit of a body blow. Wonder what his health problem is? Nothing terminal, I hope. Seems like nothing will be the same again.'

'And for you?'

'Waiting for the redundancy letter. Only a matter of time till Samson or Randall walks through that door to give me my notice. I've been a faithful servant here for many years. I hope that will stand me in good stead for the redundancy payment.'

'Any news from Fiona? Randalls, or management buyout?'

'I expect the former, now that Baker is going. I'm not sure whether we could actually manage the practice now. Hey, ho. Fancy a coffee? Nothing much else to do.'

'That would be very kind.'

She went to the kitchen and returned with a cafetiere and sugar in a Clarice Cliff bowl. Whatever Roger's faults, and there seemed to be many, he had some good taste.

'I'd take you on if I could,' I said, 'but we're fully staffed at the moment. Can I have first refusal on you, if something turns up?'

She smiled. 'You're a softy, Nick. I'm not sure how I would fit well into the world of fraud.'

'Fraud, so it seems, is the way of the world. You'd be surprised at what people can do to make a few bucks. Or a lot of big bucks.'

'Baker?' she asked, staring at me.

'My lips are sealed.'

'But you haven't denied it.'

'I know I can trust you. Wouldn't be considering you for a job if I didn't.'

'I admire your faith.'

'Coffee's good,' I said, to change the subject.

'I'm glad,' she replied, still looking shaken. 'Colombian. Got it specially for you this morning. I know how much you like your coffee. Bought the cafetiere, too.'

'I appreciate it,' I said. 'Look, I'll try to get all this wrapped up by the end of next week. Remove the uncertainty. It's the best I can do.'

'I understand. If it were to be done, best done quickly. Isn't that what they say?'

'Something like that. Any point in me speaking to the office staff?'

'Best left,' she said, shaking her head.

'What do you make of Samson?' I said. 'He seems ineffectual. No real go to the man.'

'You're right — seems to lack what we used to call good old-fashioned gumption. He's good at his job, though. Clients like him.'

'But he's not a natural leader, which is what you will need with a management buyout.'

'Who knows?' she defended.

'Indeed.'

CHAPTER TWENTY-TWO

We decided it wasn't a cooking-in day or a night for Toddy's — you can have too much of a good thing, good to keep it special — or a takeaway, so Anji, Cherry and I met up at Lee Wong's in the basement of Canary Wharf. The place was buzzing, but, out of experience, I had booked a table.

'How's a day in the life of administration executive been?' I said to Anji.

'Well, let's just say I learned a lot about making tea and coffee and flashing my neat pins to Randall. I made an excuse about tonight and promised to stay late and have dinner tomorrow.'

'Anything incriminating come up yet?' I asked.

'Not yet, but I need to talk to more of the girls there. Get a dossier down in the wire. Build up a history.'

'My work at Randalls is basically done,' said Cherry. 'A couple of people still to see, but I can have a pretty good stab at a valuation and share exchange price, although that doesn't seem relevant any longer. There don't seem to be any skeletons in the closet. Everyone knuckles down. What about Ackroyds?'

'We have a man who needlessly fiddles his expenses, one that would like to do everything for free, one who has a terrible home life and would welcome some additional money, one who would like to run the show but isn't fit for the job, and so the list goes on. Lots of motives and no concrete alibis.'

Our starters arrived — seaweed, tea-smoked chicken, honey ribs and some pancake rolls. We were quiet for a while. Then it was back to business.

'I think I'll come to Randalls tomorrow,' I said. 'Compare notes with you and take him through some preliminary figures. See if he's still sure he wants to carry on. Chase him on paying our first invoice, too.'

'Shall I stay?' Cherry asked.

'Can't do any harm. You know the background and the people. You will have crunched the figures. Seems like the best approach.'

She nodded as she slipped her fingertips into the warm lemon-drenched finger bowl and rinsed them delicately.

Anji was silent for a moment, and I guessed she was slipping her heels off.

'I'm sure Randall will hit on me tomorrow,' she now said. 'Can I have Arthur as back up?'

'Of course,' Cherry said, 'wouldn't dream of putting you in unprotected.'

'See if you can get the dinner pushed back to nine,' I added. 'I've got him watching Baker tonight. It would be good if we could give him a clean bill of health, eliminate him as a suspect for the murder or another fraud. I'd like to get Arthur on Sarah Jenkins tomorrow. There's only so much you can learn from an interview at work. There will be others to tail, too.'

Several dishes of our main course started to arrive — chilli beef, kung po chicken, noodles and a lamb hotpot. We scooped a measure into our bowls and made a pretty good fist of the chopsticks.

We left at about ten. It was a balmy evening, so we decided to walk and took the shortcut back to Island Gardens. As we went through an alleyway, we found our path blocked by two heavyset men, one white and one black. They were dressed in black jeans, T-shirts and hooded jackets. It was hard to see their faces.

Mr White was carrying a heavy jackhammer. We all froze.

'If it's all the same to you,' he said, turning to me and speaking in an eerily casual voice, 'we'll just break your fingers and be on our way.'

'And if it's not all the same to me?' I asked, trying to keep my voice even.

'We'll just break your fingers and be on our way.'

'Seems very fair,' I said. 'Means I don't have to make a difficult decision. Before you do, is there a reason for the fingers? Be nice to know what I've done to deserve it.'

'Yeah, I wrote it down.' He fished in his inside pocket and pulled out a scrap of paper. 'Message reads, keep your toes — oh, sorry, that's my bad writing — keep your nose out of our business. End of message. Hope that makes sense.'

'A bit cryptic, I'm afraid.' I took my bomber jacket off and wrapped it around my lower left arm. Cherry did the same with her black cardigan. 'Anji,' I said, 'step back where you'll be safe and call the police. Let's see what their definition of "rapid response" is like.'

I faced Mr White, the jackhammer guy, and made an effort to play for time. I had a feeling there wasn't much left, but it was worth a shot.

'I must warn you that I am a black belt in the ancient art of origami.'

'I'll bear that in mind if I ever need a paper airplane.' He tapped the jackhammer against his left hand. 'Now let's get on with it. Put your hands up against the wall.'

'No can do,' I said. 'You're going to have to earn your money.'

He tutted, advanced on me and swung the hammer. I brushed it aside with my semi-protected left arm and hit him hard on the nose. Always hit 'em on the nose as soon as you can. It makes tears fall from their eyes and blinds them for a while — that was what Arthur had told me in prison, and there seemed no reason to depart from that.

Mr Black was hanging back from Cherry, unsure about hitting a woman and wondering what she was hoping to achieve by not running for cover. He was severely under-estimating her. Countless years in the Met and courses in unarmed combat had taught her how to handle herself.

I hit Mr White again on the nose and then followed through with a swift right in the stomach: his nose broke; the stomach was too muscled to hurt. Time for a change of tactic.

I hit him again in the stomach and he doubled up momentarily. I then interlocked my fingers and gave him an uppercut under the chin with both hands which forced his head back. I glanced over at Cherry — Mr Black couldn't get close to her. Every time he advanced, she forced him back by a high kick to the chest.

I went for a straight right to his head to disorient him, but I must have telegraphed it, for he swerved out of the way. He swung the jackhammer again, and the force of the blow went through my jacket, stunning my muscles and knocking my left arm aside.

A police siren filled the air.

'This is not finished,' Mr White said, as he turned and ran up the alley, swiftly followed by his partner. 'We'll get you in the end.'

'But not today,' I shouted after him, though whether he could hear me I didn't know — he was pretty fast for a big guy. 'Are you okay?' I said to Cherry, wrapping my arms around her. She was shaking. 'You were brilliant. Keeping him at bay was the best thing you could do.'

A squad car screeched to a halt and two male police officers ran into the alley. They stared at our running assail-ants and obviously decided it wasn't worth the effort.

The rear door of the squad car opened.

Out stepped Palmer.

'Trouble seems to follow you around, Shannon,' he said.

'Sometimes it gets ahead of me, too,' I replied.

'I heard the name Anji on the call and thought it must be you.'

'Good of you to drop by, in that case.'

'My good deed for the day,' he said. 'I think we need to talk.'

'Drive us back and we'll do that.'

Anji appeared and put her arms around me. I could feel the fear coming to a head and shock kicking in. Cherry walked over and hugged her. Together we got her in the squad car, all of us packed tightly inside. One of the police officers stayed behind to search for any evidence that could help to find the assailants. I didn't fancy his luck.

'Nice pad,' Palmer said, as we entered the second floor of our home and office. I think he liked the symmetry of the three sofas. 'Must have cost a pretty penny,' he added.

'Before you get any ideas, it's not mine. Belongs to a good friend.'

I poured brandies for the three of us involved in the incident. Palmer declined the offer. Sensible. Didn't want to let his guard down. Or me to have any leverage against him. We sat down, Cherry and Anji close together on one sofa and me on another.

'Okay,' he said, 'so what's the story? What happened?'

'They must have been watching us. Picked us up as we left Lee Wong's. We made it easy for them by walking home. They were waiting for an opportunity to strike.'

'Give me some details?'

'I reckon they were bouncers aiming to get a bit of freelance money. Cash in hand. They knew what they were doing. We were just a box to be ticked. Didn't expect to meet any resistance.'

'What did they look like?' Palmer asked.

'The white guy had a broken nose and got another one tonight, but nothing more to go on. Black clothes, hoods. Stereotypes. You'll find a dozen of them outside the night-clubs every night.'

'Anything else?' he said. 'Useful, that is.'

'One had a tattoo around his right wrist, tiger, if that's any good,' Anji interjected.

'Can't do any harm, little lady,' he said.

I could feel Anji bristle. If it wasn't enough to have Randall to sort out, there was now a sexist policeman to contend with.

I took a sip of the brandy and felt the warm liquid soothing the pain in my left arm and energizing me. I knew there would be no sleep tonight.

'This all seems to be too much of a coincidence,' Cherry said. 'You can't still suspect Nick for the murder of Ackroyd.'

'Could have been a set-up,' he said. 'Carefully planned as a smokescreen.'

'Come on, Palmer,' I said. 'Get real. We need to pool our resources, not be competing with each other. What have you got so far?'

'You know I can't tell you that. What have you got?'

'I've narrowed it down,' I said.

'To whom?'

'Everybody,' I said.

'And that's supposed to help me?' he said, finally giving in and sitting down. He pulled up the knees of his trousers to stop them from getting baggy and stared at me as if seeing me for the first time.

'I think you mean well, Shannon,' he said, 'but you need to refrain from always being the joker. Work on your delivery. I ask you again. What have you got?'

'How about a swap?'

'I can't do that.'

'I'm convinced that the murder is linked to the takeover by Randalls,' I said, deciding to just tell him my thoughts. 'It's acted as a catalyst for those who want it to go through and those who don't. There are suspects on both sides. Eliminating Ackroyd changes the game plan. Richard Randall still wants it to go ahead, but there are others who would prefer a management buyout.'

'Names?'

I gave him a potted version of what little I had found during the interviews with senior people. I omitted Baker's petty fraud. I had given my word that I wouldn't tell anyone.

'I can think of circumstances where there will be clarity,' I said.

'And those are?' he said.

'If there is another murder.'

* * *

'I thought he was never going to go,' said Arthur, when he arrived. 'What did Mr Plod want?'

'Don't be too unkind,' Cherry said. 'He saved us from a bad case of broken fingers.'

'Is there a good case of broken fingers?' he asked.

I explained what had happened earlier.

'The old tricks still work,' he said, nodding in approval. 'Hit 'em on the nose. Never fails.'

'What did you find out from tailing Baker?' I asked.

'Interesting,' he said. 'Left work at six and went home to one of those mansion apartments fronting the embankment. The sort where you've got everything — swimming pool, gym, underground car park. Cost a pretty penny in rent. Either got a lot of money or feeling the pinch through overheads.'

He got up and poured a small brandy. Took a sip and shivered.

'Came out of the apartment at six thirty. He'd changed from his suit into a sports jacket and yellow cords — what every best dressed middle-aged man about town is wearing. Walked for fifteen minutes and went into a Chinese restaurant. I was feeling a bit peckish so I followed him inside. Must have been a regular. Staff were all over him. Brought him a beer before he had even sat down. He chatted with them. Slightly too long, I thought, from the reactions of the waiter — who obviously wanted to get away and serve other customers. Baker made some excuse and talked to the people

111

at the next table. Read a newspaper and was skilled with chopsticks. Even managed the seaweed.'

'What then?' Cherry asked. 'Did he clock you?'

'Clock me? He came over and talked to me. Asked if he could borrow a pen for his crossword.'

'Right. Anything else?' I asked. 'Any deductions?'

'Oh, yes.'

'And that is?'

'He's lonely. Full stop. Poor soul.'

CHAPTER TWENTY-THREE

'And how's our administration executive doing today?' I asked Anji when she brought the coffee into Randall's office. A feigned edge in my words. She was wearing a short denim skirt, an off-the-shoulder vest and above-the-knee black boots. There were veins throbbing on Randall's face.

'Why don't you join us, Anji,' he said, to rub salt in the wound. 'Don't be bitter, Shannon. It doesn't become you.'

Anji sat down. There was an expanse of leg in view.

Cherry coughed politely. 'Down to business.'

'Yes,' he said, regaining attention, 'let's talk money.'

'As it stands,' I said, 'Ackroyds is worthless. It hasn't made a profit for the last three years. The good news is that there is no tax bill to consider. But before we go on, we have to discount the offices — rent or buy, that is something for a separate negotiation between you and Fiona Ackroyd.'

I took a sip of coffee. It was foul. *Anji, what are you doing to me?* I noticed she hadn't poured a cup for herself.

'The thing that makes a huge difference to the value is Ackroyd's death,' I continued, setting my cup down. 'If you strip away his salary and other remuneration, you can add a hundred and fifty thousand to the bottom line. At a ratio of five, that makes Ackroyds' price now at seven hundred and fifty thousand.'

Anji crossed her legs. Time stood still — for Randall at least.

'Then we have synergy. The whole place is in the dark ages. Far more support staff than you need. At a rough guess, you could save another hundred and fifty thousand. Total value now climbs to one and a half million.'

'I don't see why I have to pay for synergy,' he said, dragging his eyes away from Anji. 'I'd be the one who makes the efficiencies. Ackroyds can't claim any of that.'

'But it makes the deal more attractive; Fiona will see that. Thus, we have a starting point. Straight cash, no share swap.'

'As for your value,' Cherry said, 'you have a profit history of around a million a year. That would value you, at a ratio of eight, at eight million. Any share swap would be at a rate of one share in Randalls to just around five or six shares of Ackroyds. I don't think that will sound attractive to Fiona, Baker or Samson. They'll want the cash.'

'I reckon,' I added, 'that Baker and Samson would be happy with ten per cent of one and a half million — a hundred and fifty grand each — even ten per cent of seven hundred and fifty thousand would seem like a good deal. That just leaves Fiona. I would suggest an early meeting with her, with us acting as impartial intermediaries.'

'Agreed,' Randall said. 'Set it up. Contact my PA for availability.'

'One more consideration,' Cherry said. 'What will you pay as redundancy? Some of the staff have been there for many years — twenty years for Beryl, for instance. I think Fiona will be swayed if you are generous. It will hit your bottom line in the first year, but you'll still come out on top.'

'That's up for negotiation,' he said. 'Cherry knows I don't take prisoners. Any staff not pulling their weight or excess to requirements will have to go.'

'It's going to be a culture shock,' Cherry said. 'Ackroyds' management style is to just get on with it. No direction, no interference, no pressure.'

'They'd be paid well to soften the blow of a new style,' Randall said. 'I'm effectively buying the solicitors. If they can't bring their clients, they will have to work even harder to get new ones. No passengers.'

'Another consideration,' I said, 'is that Baker has had to resign for health reasons. You'll have to work hard to retain his clients.'

'That's a blow, but we can get over that. The price goes down. Simple as that.'

'May I ask a question?' Anji said, unable to hold her tongue. 'Do you care anything for the existing staff? They're one big family. It isn't quite the same here. Don't you worry about burnout?'

'Good question, little lady.' Randall's demeanour changed completely as he addressed her. 'I'm sure you'll be an asset to us. Bit of training is all you need. Have I under-estimated you? That would be rare.'

She smiled tightly. 'And the answer to my question?'

'I employ people in the best years of their lives. When they start to wane, that's the time for them to move on and bring in some new blood.'

'Sounds like time for us to go,' I said, as Anji opened her mouth to protest. 'I'll arrange the meeting with Fiona as quickly as possible. I'll submit our final invoice at the meeting — our work will be over. We'd be grateful for prompt payment — same day, preferably. Keep everything neat and tidy.'

'Leave it with me,' Randall said. 'I'm grateful for what you have done. I'll use you again. Plenty more jobs like this. Randalls is going places, and you can join us on the journey. Show our guests out, Anji. Make sure they don't steal anything on the way.'

What a card.

* * *

'Sorry,' said Anji when we were outside the offices. 'I shouldn't have spoken. Could have blown it.'

'You got away with it,' I said. 'You can do no wrong in his eyes. Just remember in future to play dumb. The dumber the better. Don't worry that pretty little head of yours about it.'

'Hah, hah,' she said.

'Getting tricky, isn't it?' Cherry asked. 'Hang fire. Won't be much longer.'

'I just need to get those invoices paid before we expose him,' I said.

'It will mean no more business from him,' Cherry said.

'Do we want any more business from him?' I asked.

'Definitely not,' they both said.

'You had better get back, Anji,' I said. 'He'll be missing you. What's the plan for tonight? Dinner again?'

'Apparently, he has a special surprise for me.' She grimaced.

'I'll get Arthur to tail Sarah Jenkins for the first part of the evening, and then he'll stick to you like glue.

'Can you get the report completed,' I said to Cherry after we had said goodbye to Anji, 'and ready to hand to Randall, Fiona and, I suppose, Baker, and Samson as the current head of practice? Get the invoices typed up, too.'

'And what will you be doing?'

'Back to Ackroyds. There's still a murder to solve.'

* * *

Beryl made some coffee, and we sat together in Ackroyd's office out of the way of everybody. I told her I would work from here while it was empty. It was spacious, and I could have the French doors open to give a breeze. Provided I looked over my shoulder for a murderer, that is.

'Did the police search through the office?' I asked her.

'They took his personal laptop, certainly, although that wouldn't help them much. They returned it yesterday, so I doubt they found any clues.'

'Do you have his password? That would be useful. And any keys he had to the desk and the filing cabinet.'

'I'll go and get them.'

'Before you go,' I said, 'how is your husband? You said to Anji when she took you home that he was unwell. Cancer she said. Any improvement?'

'He's close to the final stage. At least I don't have to feel guilty about taking time off to be with him. I suppose I'm technically Samson's secretary now that he is head of practice, but he has his own. Basically, I'm superfluous. The only comfort for me are my two cats and even they are becoming old and frail. One sleeps all the time; the other has become incontinent. I'll soon have to bite the bullet and have them put to sleep. It never rains.'

'Money?' I asked. 'Do you need a sub? I'm sure I can arrange something from somewhere. I have Roger's access details for the system. I could do it now. Could clear it with Samson later.'

'Thank you, but I can manage for a while. At some stage, I would get some redundancy pay. Be nice to know how much, but I can manage for now.'

'Tell you what. If you're at a loose end, go to our offices and talk to Morag. She might be able to give you some advice about the future. She's a chatterbox. You'll love her. You'll enjoy her company.'

'Thank you. I think I'll do that. You're very kind.'

'I believe everybody should get what they deserve. You deserve better than sitting on Randall's scrapheap. Go to our place and take some cake and Madeira; Norman would love that.'

'I think I'll do that. Do you need anything before you go?'

'Just some more coffee and a smile.'

'Coming up,' she said smiling back.

I opened the French doors while I waited for Beryl to return with the coffee, password and keys. She brought them in and told me she had spoken to Morag and would be taking up the offer of dropping in.

I set up my laptop and Ackroyd's terminal on the conference table and went to sit at his desk. It felt strange. Just a few days ago, Roger was alive and genial as we sat opposite each other for the afternoon tea ritual. Now life had gone and left a void to be filled.

I started on the top of his desk. A paperweight in the shape of an airplane, a proper fountain pen sitting on top of some blotting paper encased in a leather frame. A photo of Fiona with their sons, their son's wives and children. I unlocked the middle drawer and found a diary. I had to start somewhere. What better place.

What was first evident was that Roger had had little to do. Few appointments in any week. In the week before his death there were only two entries with any information — 'lunch with AJ, apologize!' and 'lunch with CP, research'. There was one entry which tersely said *out* with no explanation or reason. Be good to find out what they were about. Anything special, or did he just like a good lunch?

In his desk drawers were the mundane articles of another fountain pen and two bottles of ink, one black, one red, notepad, paper clips and assorted stationery items. I put the notepad on top of the diary for studying later.

I went across to the filing cabinet, unlocked it and pulled open the top drawer. No Madeira, no glass — presumably taken by Palmer and crew for analysis. The second drawer had folders with names in plastic holders. I took them out and laid them on the desk. The third and final drawer contained what I took to be the equivalent of an out tray, a stack of files in manila pockets. Why he had these when Beryl filed everything away so efficiently, I didn't know. Maybe they were in current use. Again, I put them on the desktop.

I started with the notepad. Many of the pages contained doodles of no significance and lists of things to do — 'complete Hutchins contract', 'get cash', 'talk to Baker' and so on. Around three pages in, there was a phone number. I picked up the phone and dialled the number.

It was answered by a jolly voice which said 'Abacus Detective Agency: you can count on us.' I put the phone down.

CHAPTER TWENTY-FOUR

I wanted to spend time at Ackroyds the next day to look at the system traffic on a Friday, to see whether it was as much as everyone had said. I could work my way through Roger's files while keeping an eye on the computer terminal. I rang Abacus and arranged an appointment for the afternoon. Should be interesting. I withdrew five hundred pounds in cash on my way home. I was pretty much prepared for the day.

Now we were repeating our evening ritual of sitting in the first-floor lounge anxiously waiting for the sound of the tinny horn heralding the arrival of Anji and Arthur.

The horn sounded. In walked Anji. For tonight's dinner date she had selected a short black leather dress with a halter neck exposing her shoulders. The mic was covered by her long hair, softly curled for the night, and the recorder had needed a lot of help from Cherry to conceal. She kicked off her high-heel shoes, sighed and sat on the sofa. Morag poured her a glass of white wine and handed it over.

'Bliss,' Anji said.

'Spill the beans,' I said, seeing the arrival of Arthur. He took a beer from the fridge and sat down. 'What was tonight's fun and games?'

'We progressed to kneesy under the table, still a lot of hand touching, too.'

'All on record?' Cherry asked.

'I haven't listened yet, obviously, but it should all be there. Don't see why it wouldn't be. But you haven't heard the best of it yet.'

'Which is?' I asked.

'Apparently, I need *culture*. Part of the administration executive's job spec, but help is at hand in the presence of Prince Charming Richard. I am off to Paris next weekend. I have also been given five hundred pounds to shop for clothing and accessories, and I think I know what he has in mind. Small and lacy is my bet.' She took a large sip of her wine, sighed again and turned to me. 'How long do we have to keep this up?'

'Not much longer. Everything will be over next Friday. Don't bother about Paris. We'll have sorted everything by then. We're in the closing stages. I suggest you pull a sickie for a couple of days to take a break. No more dinner dates: tummy problems, need to get fit and well for Paris. Lay it on thick. Do you have any supporting data from the other girls at Randalls?'

'Plenty,' Anji said. 'While I'm on sick leave, I'll transcribe it all. Produce a report with lots of quotes.'

'We need to get our money before we expose Randall and maybe jeopardize the deal. I have access to all the Ackroyds passwords I need to make a payment. How about you, darling?' I said to Cherry. 'Can you do something similar for Randalls?'

'No reason not to. It's a more advanced system than Ackroyds, but I can arrange access. Shouldn't be a problem. We can hand over our reports tomorrow and take it from there. Any work we do after that can be pro bono. Any news from Fiona? When can she manage a meeting?'

'I've arranged the meeting for Tuesday. First day she could make. Why don't you see if you can attend, Anji. You've been in on it from the start. You deserve to be in at the kill.'

'I can get pretty much what I like at the moment. I think I can sort it.'

I got up and poured myself a glass of the red wine that Norman had chosen for the night. In his role as owner of Toddy's, he was able to sample wines from suppliers. Drinking with Norman was never dull. A new experience every time.

'Your turn, Arthur,' I said.

He took a swig of his beer. 'Nothing much to report. Went straight from work to a two-up, two-down house close to Stratford. Handy for commuting. I had to ditch my car to follow her. Made it harder to stay hidden, but it was OK. Didn't have to wait long outside her house. Parking on the street would have been difficult. Chock-a-block. Houses designed before everybody had three cars.

'Anyway,' he continued, 'she gets home at six fifteen. Lights on in the kitchen. Can see her through the window having a glass of wine. Lights go on upstairs. Main bedroom, I reckon. Draws curtains. Long wait where nothing happened. Must have booked a taxi because one pulls up at eight. She appears all dolled up: red jacket, leather from the shine, red skirt with a split up the side, ditto, white low-cut blouse, heels — she's a bit unsteady on them, maybe the wine or she's just unused to wearing them. Gets in the car. All prepared for a fun evening. Make that *intimate*. Dinner date with someone special. Couldn't follow the cab, but my guess it's some swanky restaurant. End of story. Back in time for watching Anji.'

'So from the dull chrysalis emerges the butterfly in all its glory,' I said. 'Last questions before bedtime. Any thoughts on Beryl? What did you make of her?'

'Lovely lady,' said Morag. 'Fascinated by the work we do. She could be an asset. I must admit I'm struggling at the moment. Business is growing so rapidly I'm finding it hard to keep up.'

'Are we sure about this?' said Norman. 'This isn't just a charitable exercise? Are we thinking this as a business solution or are we just being soft?'

'I thought she was great,' said Anji. 'From what I saw of her at my limited time at Ackroyds, she had all the skills we need.'

'Let's sleep on it,' I said. 'It wouldn't be something we could do straight away — we need to wait till she gets her redundancy money and for her home life to be settled, her husband, cats. Let's get first refusal in the meantime. Express our interest. Are we all clear on what to do tomorrow? Me, I'm back to Randalls in the afternoon — I've a criminal expert to interview.'

'I'm waiting for the estate agents to get back to me with some valuations of the offices,' Norman said.

'Reports,' said Cherry. 'Anji can observe. Be great experience.'

'Helping with the reports,' said Morag. 'Invoices a priority.'

'And,' I said, 'in the afternoon, I'm off to meet a gumshoe.'

CHAPTER TWENTY-FIVE

I unlocked the door to Ackroyd's office and sat at his desk. Beryl walked in with coffee. Mind reader.

'What did you make of us?' I asked. 'Didn't frighten you off?'

'On the contrary. I thought both Norman and Morag were lovely. And what fantastic offices. You're so lucky. I took your advice about the cake and Madeira. Norman was wowed by the gesture. Morag was a darling. We chatted for what seemed like ages. It was good to talk to someone who was sympathetic to all that was going on in my life. I hope I didn't put her too far behind with her work.'

'We would like first refusal when you are going for a job. No promises at the moment, but we're interested. Could you manage the sort of things we do? Obviously, discretion is key, but you must have that from your time working for Roger. How would you feel being under Morag?'

'No problem. She's delightful.'

'Keep me posted. Right, I'd like you to do some secretarial work for me this morning. There were two entries in his diary in the last week or so. Just initials — AJ and CP. Ring any bells?'

'AJ would be Alan Jones. Senior partner at a firm of solicitors we come across from time to time. Why he would want to meet him, I don't know.'

'It had the word *apologize* next to the time of meeting. Any clues what that might mean?'

'No, sorry.' She shook her head helplessly.

'OK. Can you book me an appointment with Jones, soon as you can? Tell him it's urgent. Keep Tuesday morning free for a meeting with Fiona and Randall. Samson and Baker need to be there, too, and Walker and Anji. Better offer coffee and tea.'

She nodded.

'How about CP?' I asked.

'Colin Priestman. Another senior partner at another firm of solicitors. Why he would want to meet him, again I don't know, but they were drinking buddies.'

'Again, please could you fix me an appointment. Urgently,' I said. 'There was another appointment that just said *out*. Did he confide in you about that?'

'Equally puzzling,' she said. 'I usually handled his diary. He wasn't very organized. Strange that he kept these secrets from me.'

I picked up one of the files in the manila folders. I passed it over to her.

'He kept these locked in the bottom drawer of the filing cabinet. Have you seen these before?'

She looked at the first file and quickly scanned the others.

'It's a file on Baker,' she said. 'I don't know why he would need this.'

'They are dossiers on all the senior staff members.'

'But I kept the personnel files, and these contain much more information.' She paused. 'I'm beginning to wonder if I knew Roger as much as I thought.'

'I'll go through them this morning, and then I'm out. I'm meeting a detective agency. Can you think of any reason why Roger had the number of a private detective?'

She shook her head. 'What's going on?'

'That's what I aim to find out.'

'Oh,' she said. 'I know who did that conveyance that was involved in the dry run. You wouldn't believe it.'

She gave me the name.

I did believe it. Fitted my hunch, although it was obvious, I must admit.

She left to start making phone calls and the arrangements for the Tuesday meeting. I set up Roger's terminal and navigated to the client account. Watched it with one eye. With the other, I picked up one of the files and started reading.

It soon became clear that we wouldn't need much more of Arthur's sleuthing. The file on Baker, for instance, was comprehensive. It covered his education (minor public school, Exeter university), bachelor (lives alone in a mansion flat), instances of dating (from an app), likes playing golf and malt whisky, drives a Mercedes.

Each file was equally detailed, much of which we knew already. There were some surprises, though. Samson's file noted that he seemed to be having a liaison with a well-dressed woman — unfortunately, not identified — and liked the slow tension of test cricket. Drives an old Saab.

The first of the money came through, in and out immediately. Transaction from Baker, authorized by Jenkins. There was then an opportunity to cancel the transaction: ninety seconds to do so.

Another transaction came up — Samson. It was authorized and went on its merry way to another firm of solicitors. It was swiftly followed by one by Seymour. They hadn't exaggerated the volume of traffic.

I spent the morning going through the files once and going through them a second time, so that I knew the people intimately. Now it was gumshoe time.

* * *

Abacus Detective Agency was on the third floor of a narrow building in St Martin's Lane. There was a pile of post in the entrance that looked like spam mail that everyone in the building obviously ignored. The stairs creaked as I climbed up. I guessed absentee landlord.

The proprietor — one Albert Archer — was sitting behind a cheap desk when I entered. He was thin, with a five o'clock shadow at one in the afternoon. He had a sharp Roman nose and reminded me of a weasel, but maybe I was being unkind. His whole appearance was shabby and unkempt. It seemed he would be better for a good meal and a new wardrobe. He looked up, but didn't offer to shake hands, for which I was grateful. I took a seat, introduced myself and slipped a business card across the desk.

'Forensic accountant,' he said. 'My tax problem must be worse than I thought.'

'I'm here to talk about Roger Ackroyd — the late Roger Ackroyd.'

'Ackroyd,' he said to himself. 'Where have I heard that name before?'

I took all the files from my briefcase, opened the top one — Baker's — and showed it to him.

'I think you prepared this and all these others for Ackroyd. It's good work. You should be proud.'

'If I did, then it would be client confidential.'

'How about I engage you for an hour?' I took out the five hundred pounds and put it just out of reach of him.

'Ah, Ackroyd,' he said. 'Now I remember him. What did you want to know?'

'Everything. From the beginning.'

'He came to see me about a month ago. He wanted dossiers on his senior staff. Said he needed to know everything about them — history, character and what made them tick. Gave no reason, and I didn't ask. Over the course of the next two weeks I followed them around and also did some research. What I found out is the product of the dossiers you have before you.'

'What was his reaction?'

'Gratitude. He signed a cheque. Big one, too. Lots of work involved.'

'Didn't say if he learnt anything?'

'No. Just went away a happy bunny. I thought that was the last I had seen of him. I was wrong. A fortnight ago, he came back. Different reason this time.'

'Which was?'

'He thought someone was going to murder him.'

He pulled open the bottom drawer of the desk and took out a bottle of cheap whisky and two glasses. It's what gumshoes do.

Archer poured two fingers into each glass and slid one across to me. It burnt my throat — it needed some ice to cut through the fire. What you get when you buy a cheap brand.

'He thought he was being watched, followed,' Archer said. 'No hard evidence, just a gut feeling, an uneasy prickling in his neck. He wanted me to tail him. See what I could find out — corroborate or eliminate. He was worried.'

'Any hard evidence? What was your view?'

'I couldn't verify. I tailed him for a week and couldn't see any signs. I even went to his office and checked for bugs. All clear. He paid me off and went away reassured.'

'With justification?'

'No one tailing him when he was walking around; no cars keeping tabs on him.'

'Could this be another reason for the staff dossiers?' I asked. 'The names on a hit list?'

'Didn't say so, but many clients don't open up completely.'

'Any guesses on who's the wrong one in the pack?'

'I'd discount the woman. Nothing unusual about her. Looked like a settled home life. Didn't display any signs of having a need for money — not driving an old banger, that sort of thing. Murder would be out of character. Though poison is a woman's weapon of choice.'

'And the men?'

'I can't see any of them capable of killing Ackroyd. Takes a lot to drive someone to murder. No strong motives that I can see.'

'I think it will be about money,' I said. 'It's always either love or money in murder, and I can't see that love would be relevant in Ackroyd's case.'

'Was there lots of money sloshing around?' he said.

'Enough,' I replied.

'Enough to kill for?'

I nodded. 'Ripe for the picking.'

'What about the police?' he said. 'What have they got that you know? Let anything slip?'

'They're clueless, but I don't hold that against them. Case is a muddle. Means, motive, opportunity. Means we know about; plenty of opportunity; motive unclear.'

'So the murderer gets away with it?'

'Oh, no. Follow the money. That will reveal all. Just a matter of time. I'll get there in the end.'

'I think you will. Here's to patience.'

* * *

I went back to Randalls in the late afternoon. The solicitor handling the criminal work there was called Steven Hayes. He was tall and imposing in a grey tailor-made three-piece suit completed by a folded blue handkerchief in his top pocket. It matched his tie, and his style could be classed as dapper, although some might say showy. He had long black hair that came over the collar of his pink shirt and a well-trimmed moustache.

His office was clinically clean of anything that might make Palmer wince. Papers and files were set out on a wide window ledge and there was only one — the current case file — on his desk. On one wall there hung a framed degree certificate — second class honours, upper division, Durham — and on another plain white wall, a poster of a Banksy. I found it hard to read any significance in it. Dilettante? Intellectual? Just to bring a little life to an unadorned office?

He shook my hand firmly and invited me to sit down in a padded leather-and-chrome chair opposite him and offered coffee from a pod machine that sat on a sideboard in the corner of the room. I wondered whether he was going to try to sell me a used car.

'Welcome,' he said. 'How can I help?'

'Just a little background,' I said. 'Tell me what you do here?'

'I handle the criminal work. Mostly defence, but occasionally prosecution. Lots of appearances in court, with or without a barrister. You meet some interesting characters. The job's never dull. Mostly my clients are guilty, and I do my best to keep them out of prison.'

'Doesn't bother you that they are guilty? No moral dilemma?'

'Someone's got to do it, so it might as well be me. The system is designed to give everybody a chance for justice — or escape it. It pays handsomely. My clients usually give me a gift on top of the fee. Hence the Banksy. A signed copy.' He pulled up the sleeve on his left arm. 'And the Rolex.'

'And the suit?' I asked.

'And the suit,' he replied.

'I'd hate to do your tax returns,' I said, smiling grimly.

'I pay my fair share of tax,' he said. 'Can I help it if my clients are generous?'

I wasn't sure the tax man would see it that way. Seemed like close to the wire to me.

'Have you been here long?' I asked.

'Seven years next month,' he replied. 'Doesn't time fly when you're having fun?'

I nodded. Exactly my sentiment. Seven years in prison went in a flash. Every day a fresh reminder of freedom lost.

'Tell me about your clients?' I said, changing the subject.

'From the gutter to the gang leaders. I deal with them all. I have a good reputation among the underworld. I'm the first port of call when they're in trouble.'

And vice versa, I wondered?

'Anyone famous or that I would have heard of?' I said.

'Doubt it,' he said. 'You've probably heard about the unsuccessful cases, but they are few. Most of the successes go under the radar. I do a lot for the North London mob: someone there is always in trouble. I stop him getting his head nailed to the floor.' He smiled. 'Only joking.'

Weren't we having fun?

'And these are people who make their money from drugs, prostitution, people trafficking and so on. No moral dilemma there?'

'Morals are just for the poor to restrain the rich. It doesn't cause me to lose any sleep at night.'

'I know that the Ackroyds' people are generalists, but what's the system here? Does anyone help out at busy times. Randall, for instance?'

'That's not the Randalls' way. Specialism is the mantra. My clients come here for me because I'm the best defence lawyer around. They wouldn't want anyone else involved. End of story.'

'Do you — how can I put this — have to do any entertaining?'

'God no!' He shook his head. 'The other way around. Regular lunches. Social events. They're heavily into amateur boxing — brutal sport — and I get invited into those sorts of things. Race meetings, too. They know the best book-ies — paradoxically, the honest ones. Occasionally, I take Randall along to make up the numbers, or as a witness or for self-protection, although there's not much he can do in that field. But I like to show him the sort of clients I deal with. Show him he couldn't do it. Overall, it's a good steady money stream. That's why I'm a partner.'

'So what do you think of the takeover of Ackroyds?'

'Just a business deal. No great shakes. Don't think it would affect my partnership dividend at the end of the year. Maybe share percentage goes down a little — although I doubt that any of staff at Ackroyds would be made partners until they have proved themselves — but should be a bigger pool. Would do good things, too, to the share value if some-one wanted to take us over. Seems like a good deal for us. If the existing staff don't cut the mustard, we'd migrate their clients gradually and then give them the sack.'

This man was all heart.

'Ackroyds does a fair share of pro bono work. Would that remain?'

He laughed. 'What do you think?'

'Stupid question,' I said.

'Good job this isn't a job interview. I'd be straight for the door.'

'And my last question. What is the question I should have asked?'

'It's usually where do I see myself in five years' time? The answer is where I am now. Dodgy morals, but stick with the Rolex. I've got everything I ever wanted, and I don't see that changing. Now,' he clapped his hands together and gave a grin, 'I'd like to do some work.'

I took the heavy-handed hint and left, looking forward to the weekend and not listening to a tale of sorrow or of bravado. A break would be good.

CHAPTER TWENTY-SIX

But life isn't always like that. I'd settle for different.

'Good morning, Anji,' I said.

'What!' She jumped and spun around.

It was Saturday morning, and I was sitting on one of the sofas on the ground floor sipping a coffee and reading through Archer's dossiers. Outside, the river was serene. Inside, obviously not.

'Something amiss?' I said, using my keen detective skills.

'Apart from Randall the Lecherous?' she said furiously. 'Yes, there is, thank you very much. Some lowlife has scammed my gran out of five hundred quid that she can ill afford. I'd like to take him by the neck, turn him upside down and use his testicles for snooker balls.'

'You best tell me more. Calmly would be good.'

'Gran had a flyer through the door. "Fed up with all that dusting? Could you make do with some ready money? Get rid of all that clutter. I buy antiques for cash". Something like that.'

'I think I'm starting to get the picture.'

'He came along and made her an offer for all her bric-a-brac. Except there was a Chinese vase among the items. Worth at least five hundred quid. Paid fifty quid for the lot.

I'd *told* her not to respond to these flyers through the door, but she saw no harm in it. Thought she was helping, because there would be less to clear when she passed away. It's not fair. These low lives shouldn't be able to take advantage of vulnerable people.'

'And does this particular low life have a name?'

'Didn't give a proper name, of course. Just called himself Jinx.'

Jinx! I'd thought I'd heard the last of him.

* * *

I first met Jinx in Chelmsford prison, but my last view of him was six months ago, with a client in a bar in the West End. Which was lucky for that person who was at Jinx's mercy and not for Jinx. Let me fill you in on the backstory, starting with the last time.

My client and I were sitting at a table for four enjoying a bottle of champagne which I had earned with a successful case for him. We were halfway through the bottle when Jinx walked in with his prospective victim, now to be known as the mark.

For someone whose success depended on being easily forgettable, Jinx's appearance, and way of comporting himself, was decidedly distinctive. You'd notice the suits first, of course. Purple sheen, royal blue (that day), maroon — anything but black, each teamed with a complementary coloured shirt and tie and a pin holding the collar stiffly in place. Most people hadn't seen a pin like that for years; it was just another way of drawing the attention away from the face.

From the age of twenty-four, when he'd first been cautioned on the street for trickery, he'd already had silver hair, but the look was by no means unsuitable. If anything, it mediated the exuberance of the rest of his appearance and lent a certain credibility to his character.

The overall effect was to draw the eye to his aesthetic appearance and distract attention from what was almost certainly an illicit activity happening in his hands or coming out of his mouth.

Jinx would tell anyone that he was born and bred in South London (although he would, of course, have said 'proper Saff London') and never used his given name, Joshua, while actually in that area. Really though, he'd grown up in Kent, and only started frequenting London when the possibilities for committing crimes in his hometown had been exhausted (which only took two occasions, one of which was unfortunately taken up with a misunderstanding with a postman who wanted to post mail in a letterbox rather than handing it to Jinx).

South London sounded a lot more grand than North Kent, and also carried that mild implication that there might be something threatening in him. London was the ultimate playground — a grand Disney world of opportunities.

Jinx wouldn't have used a term like *grifter* or *con man* to describe himself. He saw what he did as more like art, or performance. Really, he did put on a show, and people did come away with less money than they went in with after having seen something that entertained them. Still, he was hesitant to describe what he did as magic. Magic makes it seem like there's no concrete explanation of what's happening. Magic can be learnt from books.

He had earned his nickname while doing his initial venture on the other side of the law. His family were from a long line of pickpockets, and young Joshua was expected to follow in the family tradition.

To pick pockets successfully, you need a team of three. The dip selects the target, bumps into him or her and in the resulting flurry of apologies lifts the wallet or purse. This is handed on like a red-hot relay baton to the second member of the squad, the passer. In turn, the passer slips it to the final member, the runner. Who legs it as fast as is possible without arousing suspicion. The whole operation is over in a matter of seconds, the evidence a couple of hundred yards up the road before the target even knows what has happened.

This tried-and-tested method is virtually fool proof. But only virtually. Not for Jinx.

Unfortunately, Jinx had no talent for it. He could tell a captivating story — but as far as his hands were concerned, he was all butterfingers. Wallets falling out of his hands as he was dipping or being dropped en route to the passer. In the end, after a few contretemps with the law, no one would work with him. He was a jinx. Anyone who had anything to do with him got embroiled in some problems with the police. Mostly they got off, but not always. From then on, he was known as Jinx.

And here he was, schmoozing some poor mark in preparation for the kill.

I couldn't sit there and watch. It would have been too cruel, almost making me an accessory before the fact. I excused myself from my client and approached the table where Jinx sat nursing a rum and coke. His face went bright red, confirming he was up to something.

'Not seen you since prison,' I said mildly. 'What was it you were in for that time? Ah, yes, taking money from old ladies.' I turned to the mark. 'Enjoy your drink but count your fingers before you leave.'

I walked back to my table with a smile on my face and a glow in my heart, my good deed for the day done. I raised my glass of champagne and toasted Jinx as he watched his mark leave.

CHAPTER TWENTY-SEVEN

'We should take a break after this is all over,' Cherry said. 'Just a long weekend to rejuvenate ourselves.'

We had opened the doors and stood out on the small jetty watching the boats go by on the Thames.

'Somewhere by the sea,' I said. 'Water can be so peaceful. Just looking out over the river this morning is helping to clear my mind.'

'What are we going to do about this Jinx character? For Anji's sake, and her gran's, we have to square things up. Deal out some kind of justice.'

'I already have something in mind.'

'Which is?'

'Those that live by the sword must die by the sword.'

'Is that the most you can tell me?'

'I'm still working on it, but I know one thing.'

'Which is?'

I smiled at her. 'Chinese vases will be his downfall. Oh, and something else. It's going to be a whole lot of fun.'

* * *

I made myself a coffee and some red bush tea for Cherry, who was on a health kick at the moment. This generally meant eating like a bird and shouting grumpily at people. During these times, we kept out of her way out of self-preservation.

We had settled on Norfolk on the northern coastline based at Cromer. Do the beaches and all the touristy things — fish and chips, candy floss, amusement arcades, rock with a name going through. The Beamer could do with a run after the short and slow trips in London, and we would both benefit from the wind in our hair.

'If I'm right,' I said, 'we're reaching the end game on the Ackroyd-Randall job. Even though, it seems, Roger wasn't as nice as I originally thought — lots of weak points have come to the surface during our investigation. I still feel sorry for the man. So close to retirement after building up the business — it could have been him walking along the beach with the sand through his toes.'

'I'm conflicted,' she said, sipping at her hot tea. 'We both — no, we all — know that the takeover of Ackroyds is going to be a disaster. Too big a culture shock for survival, yet we know that we have to recommend it. The figures speak for themselves. At our valuation, there's no way that the staff can afford a management buyout. So the solicitors will be worked like dogs, and the office staff will be cut to the bone. That means people like Beryl and Nancy on reception will be the first to go. All of those years of loyalty lost overnight: it all counts for nothing.'

'What if the reason for the murder — the elusive motive — was to stop the takeover going ahead? Some dark soul trying to save the happy family and dishing out what they saw as rough justice.'

'But,' I said, 'we know that Ackroyds is ripe for picking. The financial system has more holes than a colander. If you were looking at doing a fraud, now is the optimum time. Strike while the hiatus of takeover is iron hot.'

'Are we being paranoid?' Cherry asked. 'Are we relying too much on past experience than assessing this situation as an outlier? Thinking too dark; casting doubts where none should exist?'

'I think I need you on Monday. I hope to have two meetings. Will you come and watch over all the transactions that are made? We need to be alert this week. Ever watchful. If something's going down, it will happen this week.'

'Prime suspect is Sarah in Accounts, I suppose. She's the one with the power. Only she and Ackroyd can — or could in his case — authorize payments. Is she capable of murder?'

'As my private detective friend said, poison is a woman's weapon. She has to be top of our list. Opportunity, as much as anyone else. Motive, money — she knows the figures going in and out. Must be tempting. Means? It's easy to get hold of strychnine — buy some fertilizer and boil it down to a concentrated solution. She ticks all the boxes.'

'And,' Cherry said, 'what about the others?'

'I'm almost certain that she worked with an accomplice who did the murder.'

'If only almost certain, what about the others?'

'To be honest, I don't like any of them. Wouldn't be sad to see any one of them in chokey.'

'Well, should be all over after Tuesday.'

'More or less.'

'Last Friday of the month?' she said.

'You got it.'

CHAPTER TWENTY-EIGHT

In prison, Jinx had been the wide boy who claimed to be able to get you anything — *claimed* being the operative word. Once you'd handed him the money for a phonecard, some special cigarettes rather than roll ups, a takeaway curry — a speciality of Chelmsford, lifted over the wall — whatever, there was always some problem. You needed to pay that little bit extra to get what you had actually asked for and agreed to. But Jinx was always very nice about it. Charm the birds from the trees, Jinx could. At times he even had the governor hoodwinked.

Take the case of what became known as 'The Curious Incident of the Inter-Wing Football Match' in the folk-lore of Chelmsford prison, or more simply *The Match*. To understand fully such matters, you need some context. More problems occur in prison, more violent acts are committed, through boredom than any other factor. Which was why Jinx got approval from the governor to stage the match. Not only would the match itself be a break from the monotony of everyday life, but it would generate other diverting events — practice, training, strategy talks and, of course, betting, with Jinx running the books.

Managers were appointed for each wing and team selection and training started. A Wing and B Wing were pretty evenly matched, so it was a surprise when Jinx announced the starting odds. He made A Wing odds-on favourite and B Wing outsider at three-to-one. Money, cigarettes, tobacco, phonecards and anything else tradable poured in for B Wing at such generous odds.

'What can I put you down for?' Jinx asked, as he entered the cell I shared with Norman. Bunk beds — Norman on top, me below — a small table and two chairs, a couple of wall cupboards in which to stow the few personal possessions. It was all packed into a space around ten foot by eight. With Jinx here, it felt crowded. Although he always had that effect on me.

He stood there invading our personal space dressed in the regulation jeans and matching denim jacket. He tapped a black boot on the floor.

'Well?' he pressed.

'Nothing from me,' Norman said.

'Make that double for me,' I said.

'What's the matter with you two? Do you want to be the only people here not to have a chance of making a profit? There's good odds on B Wing. They're bound to go down. Faint heart and all that. What's the problem? Don't you trust me?'

'Perceptive, isn't he?' Norman said.

'Not all bad then,' I said.

'I wouldn't go that far,' Norman added.

'I'm deeply hurt,' Jinx said.

He had a habit of making a strange manoeuvre of moving his neck the way a duck does when trying to swallow a piece of bread that was too big. It was what poker players call a tell. He made it whenever he was lying. He made it a lot.

'What's he up to?' asked Norman when Jinx had exited.

'Whatever it is, he wants everyone to bet on B Wing. He must think A Wing is going to win.'

'Unless it's a double bluff,' Norman said.

'From Jinx?'

'I stand corrected.'

'Let's go and watch them training. You can never have too much information where Jinx is concerned.'

* * *

'Right back's a bit tasty,' said Norman, after we had watched training for a while.

'Know a lot about footballers?' I asked.

'Nothing,' he said, 'but I know a lot about thugs. I wouldn't want to be up against him. Who is he?'

'B Wing's answer to the Incredible Hulk. Name's Jarvis — eighteen months for burglary. Rumour has it, he got stuck in a doorway. IQ slightly smaller than his weight in stones.'

The day of the match was a Sunday, and play started immediately after the visiting hour. As soon as the last relative or friend went out through the gate, everyone assembled on the patch of grass that served as the pitch. The teams came out and were met with silence. Everyone stared at the new arrival for A Wing. That was Jinx's bit of magic. Farrell Dean — recently with Everton and their star winger — sentenced, we were to find out, to a year in prison for tax evasion. And Jinx had somehow found out about it before everyone else.

It was predictable. Two evenly matched teams until Dean had the ball. He sped down the left wing, sold Jarvis a dummy and sent a curling ball into the top corner of B Wing's net. One-nil soon became two as Dean this time rounded Jarvis by cutting inside and burying the ball low to the keeper's right. By half-time, A Wing were four goals up and the crowd was getting restless. Jinx was rubbing his hands together.

But he hadn't counted on Jarvis.

Belittled by Dean's trickery, Jarvis changed tactic as Dean approached him again and made no attempt to get the ball. He went for Dean's leg instead. I swear you could hear the bone crack on the touchline.

They carried Dean off on a stretcher from the prison hospital and an ambulance was called. While he was being taken to hospital, Jarvis shouted out, 'Well, are we playing football or not?'

Probably not, judging by his actions, but no one dared point that out to him.

The referee awarded a free kick and the game got underway again. From that point, there was no contest. Who in Hell's name was going to get near Jarvis? B Wing won by five goals to four, and Jinx was lumbered with a big payout. They carried Jarvis, their conquering hero, off the field on their shoulders to cheers and applause.

Jinx had lived up to his name again.

And Norman? He'd backed B Wing at odds of twenty to one at half-time when they were four goals down. As Jarvis passed him, the two of them exchanged winks. No one gets the better of Norman where money is involved. Jinx didn't stand a chance.

CHAPTER TWENTY-NINE

Monday morning dawned, and it was back to Ackroyds, where I was anticipating a busy day if Beryl had managed to set up the two meetings. She followed me in, carrying what had come to be the ritual cafetiere of coffee.

'You have Alan Jones at ten, and then Colin Priestman for lunch at twelve thirty. It should work out to the minute. Priestman has booked a table at his club, so I hope you're not hungry. Dire food. School dinners. Even Roger found it stuffy.'

'How was your weekend?'

'I shouldn't be such a worrier,' she said, ignoring my question. 'When there's nothing you can do about something, you should just accept it. Do the best you can. The timing with Randalls should turn out to be just right — let me spend my time at home when he gets rid of me. Only then can I move on.'

'Why don't you come with me to see Jones? Take your mind off things. It may turn out to be a complete bore, but it can't be any worse than sitting here twiddling your thumbs with nothing to do and dwelling on things.'

'Do you think he will mind?' she asked, looking hopeful.

'I don't see why. If he's willing to talk to me, what difference would it make that you are there?'

'Then I'd love to come. Could be exciting. Like in a detective programme. Looking for clues. That is what we'll be doing?'

'Always looking for clues, me. Come on. Let's finish our coffee and be off. Just one thing. Where the hell are we going?'

* * *

The solicitors where Jones worked was in northeast London in Ilford. The Beamer ate up the miles like it was imitating a tortoise. The rush hour traffic lingered and hemmed it in whatever road it was on. We parked in the nearest spot and spent ten minutes walking from there. The Victorian building sat on the corner of the high street and stood solidly as every solicitors' office should.

Jones met us in reception in his shirt sleeves, its cuffs shortened by those elasticated steel bands that I hadn't seen for a decade. He must have been in his fifties, his hair was greying, but still flourished in a style that left him having to keep scraping it out of his eyes. I had a feeling that this was a man with whom Ackroyd could have done business. I introduced myself and Beryl.

'So nice to meet you, Beryl. Roger was always talking about you. He used to say he couldn't function without you. Did he still have that afternoon habit of cake and Madeira? Old school, was Roger. The profession will miss him. Not many characters left nowadays.'

'We're trying to piece together Roger's last few weeks,' I started to explain.

'How does that work out with police?' he asked. 'Surely that is their job?'

'Let's just say we're assisting them with their inquiries.'

'Officially?'

'Not exactly.'

'So, you're sleuthing on your own account?' he said wryly.

I nodded. 'I don't have as much faith in the police as I should. Can't seem to get on with the detective in charge.

Doesn't seem to have done enough digging. Not interviewing you is one example.'

'He spent less than ten minutes with me,' Beryl said, 'and I knew Roger best of all.'

'Where do I fit in with this picture?' he said. 'I'm clearly not a suspect in Roger's murder, so what do you want of me?'

'We found from his diary that he had a meeting arranged with you shortly before his death. Can you tell us what that was about?'

'It was something trivial,' he said, 'but it caused a big problem at the time. We had a client who was buying a one-and-a-half-million-pound house in Knightsbridge. It was part of a lengthy chain, and you know if one link is broken, the whole chain breaks. On completion day, the money for one house in the chain was sent to Ackroyds at noon, but they didn't send it on till 4 p.m. Client wasn't happy hanging around for four hours with nothing happening, but there wasn't anything he could do. So we get the flack.'

'Do you know who handled it at Ackroyds?'

'He didn't say. Roger said it was his role to sort it out and he took full responsibility. That's why he came here. He felt I deserved a personal apology rather than a phone call or email.'

'Did he mention the takeover by Randalls at all?' I asked. 'Say anything about it?'

'No, but he looked worried. He seemed far away, as if something was on his mind. Didn't smile much, and I took it that that was because of the circumstances — eating humble pie. He left saying we should have lunch when the dust had settled.'

'Nothing else?'

'No. Except he brought me a bottle of Madeira as a peace offering. He was kind like that. As I said, he was a real gentleman.'

'Thank you so much for your time,' I said. I stood and shook his hand. He air-kissed Beryl and we walked out and back to the car.

'You know your next task, Beryl?'

'Find out who handled that completion.'

I smiled. 'You'll fit in just fine.'

* * *

I decided I would walk to Priestman's club in Pall Mall and get some fresh air and reacquaint myself with the shops and department stores. I was thinking of getting a gift for Cherry, Anji and Morag to celebrate the end of the job. I had nothing in mind and hoped to get some inspiration. Inspiration is always the key to unlock a puzzle.

The streets were busy. Tourists and locals taking advantage of the shops and department stores with their wide range and deals to be done on discounts in the electronics shops. I walked on the outside of the pavement against the traffic, but it was slow going.

I was daydreaming, thinking of the weekend we had booked on the Norfolk coast and all we could do there, when all of a sudden, I felt a big push on my back. I lost balance and was propelled into the road in front of an oncoming taxi. I was lucky that timing was on my side. I landed on the bonnet of the taxi and rolled up the windscreen. I managed to take hold of a wing mirror to stop myself from sliding down and finishing up under the taxi's wheels.

'You want to look where you're going, mate,' said the taxi driver.

I apologized, though wasn't quite sure what I was apologizing for. I peeled myself off the bonnet and stood up.

'That man pushed you,' said a woman, pointing up the street at a disappearing figure. 'I saw him do it.'

There was no chance of catching him up.

'What did he look like?' I asked the woman.

'He had his back to me,' she said. 'He was white, that's about all I could tell.'

'Height?' I asked.

'He was tall,' she said.

I looked more closely at her. She couldn't have been much above five foot. Everyone would be tall to her. Stupid question.

I brushed myself off as best I could and continued my walk, knowing at least one thing for certain.

Someone was trying to take me out of the game.

* * *

A man who looked like he had been a sergeant major in the army welcomed me at the club, taking a long look at my dishevelled jacket and wondering whether he should let me in. He patted me down before he let me pass the hall. He was wearing a tailcoat as part of his uniform — grey pinstripe trousers and dress shirt. He pointed the way to the restaurant. Priestman had already arrived, he told me.

The dining room had polished wooden tables and place mats of historical figures. Mine turned out to be Churchill. The room was panelled to waist height and gave the restaurant a sombre feel. This was not a place for parties.

Priestman was sitting at a table by one of the windows where you could watch passers-by through the net curtains. He stood and we shook hands. He was short with a beer belly pressing against the buttons of his black jacket. He wore a white shirt and what I took to be the club tie — a clash of stripe colours that no other institutions would pick.

'So kind of you to treat me to lunch,' he said grinning.

It was the first I knew of it.

'My pleasure,' I said, trying not to grit my teeth.

'I've ordered for you,' he said. 'Potted shrimps as a starter and the roast mutton from the trolley — one of their specialities. It's not done to talk business until after the mains, so tell me all about yourself.'

This is going to take forever, I thought.

'Apart from what you read in the media, what do you want to know?'

'Tell me about prison.'

'Grim. Next question?'

'No, really, what was the worst bit?' he pressed.

I realized I was sulking for having to pay the bill and not getting the chance for exercising my right to choose what I had to eat. *Get a grip, Shannon.*

'Claustrophobia. Being locked up most of the time. Four walls closing in on you. I'm still trying to get to grips with it. Had counselling. Seems to have helped. Don't like lifts but can just cope with them now.'

'And the inmates? As bad as one can imagine?'

'Worse.'

The starters arrived giving me the opportunity for a break in the inquisition. The potted shrimps were as liver-destroying as one expects. Basically, butter with a bit of fish. Served with French toast that shattered when you tried to smear the shrimps on them. I decided to switch from defence to attack.

'How about you?' I questioned. 'What's life as a solicitor like?'

'Grim,' he said with a smile. 'This is the most excitement I've had for many a year. Everyone complains about all the legalese that goes into small print with no punctuation. We have to write that stuff. Soul destroying.'

'And how long have you been doing this?'

'Thirty-plus years.'

'So it can't be that bad.'

'You get used to it. Death by a thousand cuts. Like most of the people in our profession, you dream about retiring to somewhere hot and sunny. Life on the deck of your boat, gin and tonic in hand while watching the sun go down.'

The mains arrived. A silver-domed trolley to add to the mystique of the fabled roast mutton was wheeled to our table. More fat to add to the shrimps. Arthur would make me do a five-mile run to shake off some of the calories.

The waiter slid back the dome and carved slices of fatty mutton on to plates and added roast potatoes, a puddle of mint sauce and some sludge of a green vegetable which I took to be overcooked spinach. Yum.

'Pudding?' Priestman asked when I had exhausted the ways of cutting fat off the edges of the mutton and eaten the minuscule amount of meat left behind. 'They do very nice spotted dick.'

I'm sure they do.

'Couldn't eat a morsel more. Fine fare. Can we now talk business?'

He nodded. 'Perfectly acceptable. What do you want to know?'

'You had a meeting with Roger shortly before he died. Can you tell me what that was about?'

'Not a believer in Mr Plod?' he said.

'Not exactly. The meeting with Roger?' I pressed.

He made a non-committal noise. 'He wanted a chinwag. Bit of advice. We dined here.'

Good job they had discounted suicide. Would have had a motive. This was like pulling teeth.

'What advice in particular?' I asked.

'He was having second thoughts about Randalls. Asked my opinion. What did I know of Randall, for example.'

'Why second thoughts, do you know?'

'He was losing faith in Randall. Thought that the heritage of Ackroyds would be gone through one signature on a bit of paper. All those years of trading lost in a wave of redundancy. Swallowed up by the machine that was Randalls' leviathan. He asked my opinion of Randall. What did I know, what had I heard on the grapevine.'

'So what did you tell him?'

'That Randall was a smug bastard who would sell his granny for a fast buck. That his nickname of Tricky Dicky was appropriate. He was ruthless. Don't trust him an inch. It was then that he decided on employing you. Get an independent view of proceedings and the valuation rather than having any input — any googly being bowled — from Randall. Smart move, I told him.'

'Did you get the feeling that that was all he was worried about?'

'In view of his murder, you mean?'

'Did he have any premonition of what might take place?'

'He was edgy,' Priestman said thoughtfully. 'Kept looking round the room as if he was sizing everyone up. I thought he was being paranoid, but I have to wonder now in the light of his death. Poison, the police say.'

'Drank his last of Madeira,' I said.

'Randall involved?'

'Not directly.'

'Inside job, do you think?' he asked.

'Has to be. He had no visitors that afternoon,' I said.

'Thrilling,' he said.

'Not for Ackroyd,' I said.

* * *

It was while I was walking back that I had the germ of an idea on how to get revenge on Jinx. What is it, I thought, that everyone loves on TV? Two areas. Cooking and antiques. The former didn't seem to provide many lucrative avenues, although it did teach me how to pronounce quinoa, so the latter would need to be the solution. The kernel of the idea was that the average viewer knows how to spot an item from the Clarice Cliff Bizarre range at twenty paces, and that the market for Chinese items was very strong, as their citizens bought back their heritage. The principle on which our scam would be built was that a little knowledge is a dangerous thing. The accompanying thesis was that you can always trust a little old lady.

I phoned Morag and asked if she could work the new high-definition camera she had bought. 'No problem' was the answer. First hurdle cleared. I then said that she needed to go to an antiques shop or try Portobello Road and gave her a list of what she needed to buy, including the cheap Chinese vase. She was to take a photo of the vase and get Anji to put it on eBay as part of a wish list from a fictitious Lee Ho. The message was to say that he would pay £10,000 for a pair of the vases. The word *pair* had to be stressed. Not one, but two.

Very important. And make sure that if someone was looking for a Chinese vase, the first result from the search would be our ad. Then to cross her fingers.

When back at Ackroyds, I asked Beryl if she and Nancy could spare ten minutes after work. The arrangement was made.

'Okay,' I said, when the three of us were together in Ackroyd's office, 'I have a favour to ask. I want to tell you a story. A story of a bad man who swindles old ladies. With your help, we can give the story a happy ending.'

I was to unleash two very astute ladies on Jinx. Something told me he didn't stand a chance.

CHAPTER THIRTY

Back in Docklands, we all sat in my office working through the papers and plans for tomorrow's meeting on the takeover. We had copies of the valuation report for everyone that was attending.

I was still worried about the attacks on us and who was behind them. The bruises on my arm were beginning to turn purple, serving as a visible reminder of what had happened in the street. It was time for Arthur to shadow us wherever we went and we decided to stick together as much as possible, so that there was only one group to watch over.

I wanted to discount Randall as a possible murder suspect to fit into the inside job theory, so turned to Anji.

'Tomorrow, try to get Randall talking about his criminal work if he dabbled in that, defence in particular. See if he knows anyone who would do a favour for him and rough us up. Randall could have hired someone for that. The other possibility is that he is working with the murderer who is inside Ackroyds. None of us trust him, so we might as well do a bit of digging.'

'I'm sure I can get him talking,' Anji said. 'He likes blowing his own trumpet.'

'Cherry,' I said, 'give them our final invoices and pay them before you come to the meeting. I'll do the same with Ackroyds. That's our fee sorted. Prepare additional invoices with a blank for whatever the amount might be for frauds found or prevented.'

'There's Baker's fiddle,' Cherry said, 'but I can't think we could charge for that without getting him in trouble. That would break our promise.'

'And why can't we do that, Anji?' I asked.

'Because it would be without honour,' she replied.

'Exactly,' I said. 'You've learnt a lot these last few days.' I paused. 'God, I hope that didn't sound patronizing. What I meant was, you've done everything we have asked, and you've done it superbly.'

'Thanks,' Anji said, 'and it did sound patronizing, but I'll forgive you.' She grinned then frowned. 'I'm more concerned about Friday and my trip to Paris.'

'Well,' I said. 'I have an idea about that.'

I outlined the idea, although still forming in my mind, and Morag clapped her hands and said, 'Bravo. I'll organize everything. I just need some contact details.'

'I'll get those to you first thing in the morning,' Anji said. 'Do I get to keep the five-hundred-pound spending money?'

'You can buy us a drink at Toddy's,' Norman said.

I knew some way that at least part of the money would finish up in his pocket. Wily creature.

'So when should we celebrate?' Norman asked.

'Friday,' I said. 'It's always been Friday. That's when it all happens. I might even let Palmer in on the act if he's a good boy. Serve our murderers up on a plate.'

'Murderers, plural?' he asked.

'Of course. Remember the guy with the jackhammer reading out the note? "Keep your nose out of our business". *Our* not *my*.'

'Do we know who this pair is?' said Anji.

'Friday will tell for certain, but we have enough detail on the trial run — the delay of the transaction that Ackroyd felt he should apologize for — to pin them down and send them off to clink,' I said. 'Justice should be done.'

CHAPTER THIRTY-ONE

We assembled at the conference table in Ackroyd's office at 11 a.m. I put Fiona at the head of the table and Baker and Samson with their backs to the French doors, Cherry, Anji and I on the other side and Randall at the other end so that he could polish his ego and consider himself as head. For form's sake, as we had run through the crucial numbers the day before, I dished out copies of the valuation report to everyone while Beryl served coffee and tea and discreetly left.

For the occasion, Fiona was wearing a smart black pin-striped trouser suit over a white blouse. The only adornment was a silver necklace with a single, but large, pearl hanging from it. Baker and Samson had on the obligatory dark-blue suits and white shirts: Samson with a matching tie and Baker one with a tiger print. I read nothing into his choice except maybe a last fingers-up to the system before he left. Cherry was wearing a light grey dress which emphasized the dark pools of her eyes. Anji, for Randall's sake, was wearing a short dark-blue skirt and a contrasting light-blue blouse through which her black bra could be seen if you looked intently, which was what Randall was doing.

'So sorry to hear you are leaving,' Randall said to Baker. 'We'll miss you.'

No one believed him.

'Don't worry about understanding this by the way, little lady,' Randall said to Anji. 'Just watch how business is done.'

I could see Anji bristling, but it went unnoticed by Randall. Hang on in there, Anji, I thought. It will all be right in the end.

I talked everyone through our valuation of Ackroyds and then Cherry did the same for Randalls. Fiona was expressionless and Randall looked smug.

'Can we start with the realization that this is not a merger but a takeover?' I began. 'Then we can move on.'

No one dissented.

'I can only go to six hundred thousand,' said Randall. 'I think that's fair.'

Fiona glared at him. 'The whole point of getting Shannon involved was for an independent valuation, so we could do away with horse trading.'

'Fine. I can go to six fifty,' Randall said.

Fiona gathered up her papers, got up from the table and walked to the door.

'Wait!' Randall cried. 'I may have been too hasty.'

What a good example he was setting for Anji about how business was done.

Fiona walked slowly back to the table and sat down. 'We start at seven fifty,' she said, 'and then talk about the second scenario.'

'Which is?' said Randall.

'The valuation taking account of synergy, for which we read the culling of staff.'

'But surely that should accrue to me, as I will be melding the two practices together,' Randall said. 'I will be the one making the difficult decisions on who stays and who goes.'

Baker piped up in support of Fiona. 'You will be getting the immediate windfall that accrues, because our ratio is five and yours is eight — that's a sixty per cent margin before you have to do anything. We should bear that in mind.'

'Hear, hear,' said Samson.

Gosh, the man can talk after all.

'I can see Randall's point, but only to a certain extent,' I said. 'To me, a nice round million sounds about right.'

'A million?' Randall gasped, staring at me.

'I tell you what,' said Fiona, 'I'll make the redundancy payments out of our share. We will be more generous than you, I would think. See the staff treated as they deserve. Make the payments to reward their loyal service.'

'That would seem to be a significant saving to you,' said Cherry to Randall. 'My advice would be to take the offer.'

'You all seem to be ganging up on me,' whined Randall.

'We're only looking after your best interest,' I said firmly. 'You'd still be half a million better off from the synergy.'

'What about these offices?' he said. 'What are they going to cost me? They were always a crucial part of the deal.'

'I suggest,' Fiona said, 'that we get three independent valuations from estate agents who specialize in this type of property. Get numbers for buying or renting and take the average of the three.'

'Sounds like a good solution to me,' I said. 'So a million pounds and the three shareholders in Ackroyds foot the bill for redundancy in proportion to their shareholding.'

'I'll go along with that,' said Baker.

'Me, too,' said Samson.

'All we need,' Fiona said, 'is for this to put it all in a legal contract. Surely that can't be hard to do.'

'I'll do it,' said Samson. 'How about a signing ceremony on Friday?'

'Cherry and I will look through the document and act as witnesses,' I said.

There were nods around the table.

'One last thing,' I said. 'Our fees.'

I handed the invoices to Randall and Samson.

'Don't worry about putting through the payments,' I said. Randall gave a smile. 'We've already done that for you using the access to the accounts you gave us for our work.'

'Isn't that a bit presumptuous?' Randall spluttered.

'Anyone not happy with our work?' I asked.

They shook their heads.

'Then there should not be a problem with our fees being paid,' said Cherry serenely. 'May I draw your attention to the note at the bottom of the invoice? According to the terms of our original contract, we reserve the right to charge an additional fee of ten per cent of any frauds found or prevented.'

'But you haven't found anything,' said Randall.

'Not yet,' I said. 'We will cease working for you at the close of play after the contract signing on Friday. Till then, we're still on watch.'

'I will abide by the terms of the original contract,' Fiona said. 'Morally, and legally, that is the right thing to do.' She gathered up her papers, walked to the door with the exit of, 'I declare this meeting over.'

Exit. Pursued by a bear? No, just Randall. Followed by a conscientious Anji.

* * *

At lunchtime, we gathered Beryl and Nancy together and tutored them in what they should say and how they could act — Nancy tonight and Beryl the following day. They were nervous, naturally, seeing that neither of them had done any acting. Cherry and I had work to do when everyone had left the office. I checked with Beryl about locking up and she said the cleaners did that. So it was just a case of whiling away a couple of hours' time.

I set up Ackroyd's computer and showed Cherry how to log on and access the accounts package. Always good to have a backup. From there, it was just a case of navigating to the clients' bank account. We watched in real time the transactions that Sarah was making.

We split up when the offices were clear, each with our own list of people. Our aim: find the details of any conveyances set to be completed on Friday. That was the day most likely to be targeted by our fraudsters.

I started off with Samson while Cherry took Baker. Samson's office was neat and tidy; it was easy to find what I wanted. Manila files were set up on the right side of his desk, overlapping so that the names of the client showed. I opened each in turn and copied down the details — name of client, name of solicitors and their bank account details.

As a final check, I went through the desk drawers. In the topmost drawer was a framed photo from his wedding. Rictus grins and a very plain white dress. In the second drawer were folders of other clients and items of assorted stationery. In the bottom drawer, in protected plastic covers, a collection of Marvel comics. Strange. Avid collector, it told me, but little else. Fight for justice?

From Samson, I went to the office of Carlton Seymour. Being the main solicitor for conveyancing, his pile was bigger, twelve in all, all stacked neatly. They were arranged in alphabetical order by client name for quick reference. The top drawer of his desk contained the usual pile of assorted stationery, including three different colours of sticky notes. The second drawer down had a collection of paperbacks, mostly published in the sixties and largely consisting of beat poets. An odd choice for one so young. I guessed he would have some discs or tapes of early Dylan albums. This was the office of a dreamer.

The bottom drawer contained only one item — a hip flask. I unscrewed the top and took a sniff. Rum. The sweet Jamaican variety. In dull moments — or, I suppose, duller than average considering his occupation — he could read a few poems and take a restorative sip. I wondered if anyone had noticed the smell of rum on his breath. Then another thought occurred to me. Being a lover of sweet drinks, perhaps he would appreciate Ackroyd's Madeira more than most.

Cherry met me in the main office. 'All done.'

'Any surprises?' I asked.

'Baker had a bottle of malt whisky and a stash of indigestion tablets,' she said. 'Kirby had some Kendal mint cake, two packs of cigarettes, a Zippo lighter and some spare fuel. He's got a sweet tooth and is a heavy smoker.'

'Okay, time to go,' I said. 'Lots to do tomorrow. Busy, busy from here on in.'

'Mixed with periods of boredom,' she said.

'There's always Jinx to keep us occupied.'

'The game's afoot,' she said.

'Amen.'

CHAPTER THIRTY-TWO

Nancy's house was a thatched cottage in the outskirts of Romford. It was large and detached, with an L-shaped conservatory added on at the side and back; I knew it would get Jinx licking his lips. It spoke of money. I carried the box with everything inside to the front door and Cherry pressed the bell. Nancy opened the door and gestured us inside. She was wearing her equivalent of mufti — a pair of grey slacks and a white top.

'Come in, Nick,' she said. 'I was just doing a spot of gardening before your friend Jinx arrives.'

I was regretting giving so much information to Beryl and her.

'Remember not to call him Jinx. There's no name on the flyer, so just avoid addressing him by name. Any name, okay?'

'Sorry, Nick. I'll remember, don't you worry.'

She showed me into the drawing room — 'lounge' being far too modern a term for this house — where a dining table for six people had been cleared.

'I thought you could put the things on this table and I'll say I've prepared the things I want to sell — just like you told me.'

I put the box on the tabletop and started emptying it. I put all the cheap tat that Morag had bought from a junk shop on to the table and looked around the room. There was a mantlepiece above a wood-burning stove. I removed the clock that was sitting in the middle and put the Chinese vase in its place. Perfect. Unobtrusive, yet Jinx wouldn't miss it.

'How about a cup of tea to help you relax while we do one final rehearsal?' I asked.

Handily, the kitchen was just off the drawing room and, with the door open a crack, it would provide an ideal place for us to listen in on what was happening.

Nancy made tea using an old-fashioned whistling kettle placed on top of a range. While she was doing so, I looked out of the window into a garden bursting with colour — red roses in bloom and other assorted flowers beyond my knowledge; I thought I could smell a touch of jasmine coming through the open window. The tea was hot and sweet and we drank it while she ran through her patter. Ten minutes later, the bell sounded and Nancy went to answer the door and let Jinx inside. I closed the door all but a few inches and was ready if she needed me — she could propose a cup of tea if things started to go wrong and step into the kitchen to consult me.

'I hope you found us okay,' Nancy said. 'We're a bit off the beaten track.'

'No problems, Mrs er . . . ?'

'Just call me Nancy. Now, I don't want to waste your time, so I've laid everything out here. You did say you bought things to help with dusting. It's a bit of a chore with me at my age. Not as strong as I used to be. Bit of rheumatism, too.'

There was a silence while Jinx was viewing the items.

'The tea pot is plate not silver, I'm afraid, so that knocks its value. The other things are very much out of fashion. I can only offer fifty quid.'

We'd paid a hundred and fifty, so there was a small profit for him. Wouldn't be a wasted journey.

'Oh dear,' Nancy said. 'But if they're worth nothing, I might as well sell them now and clear a bit of space. I'd like cash, please, to save me having to go to the bank.'

I imagined Jinx's eyes roving round the room while he dug money from his wallet.

'What about this vase?' he said.

Bingo!

'Oh, that's worth a lot — about a thousand when I last had it valued for the insurance. I could get ten thousand for it, if I ever found the other half of the pair. I'll hang on to it, thank you.'

'Suit yourself, Nancy, dear. You know where to come if you change your mind. By the way, how did you come across my name?'

This was the sticky bit — we needed to be vague here.

'It was someone at the WI. Can't remember who, she had your leaflet, said that you'd helped a friend out who needed some money. You can't beat going on personal recommendation, I find. Let me see you out.'

A moment later, the door closed, and I heard a huge sigh from Nancy. I walked back in the room and saw her smiling.

'You were great, Nancy,' I said. 'Exactly to the script. I could virtually hear his mouth watering. Now I need to borrow that vase for phase two.'

'You are really fun, Nick. Life was dull till you arrived.'

'Let's not get carried away. You've got one more meeting with him to come still.'

'What shall I do with the fifty pounds?'

'Treat yourself to a new outfit. Or maybe spend it on a meal out. Consider it your fee for being a brilliant actor. Now I'll just take the vase and get out of your hair.'

'How do you know he'll take the bait?' she asked.

'I know Jinx better than he knows himself. He'll be straight on the internet googling Chinese vases. Then we hit him with the second hook — Beryl next time.'

'I'll be ready anytime you need me.' She smiled at me. 'You know, I think I'll have a small gin and tonic to celebrate.'

'Make it a large one. You deserve it. See you tomorrow.'

What will tomorrow bring? I thought. Would Jinx take the bait?

CHAPTER THIRTY-THREE

The following morning Anji set off on her tempting of Randall. She didn't look pleased.

'I can't wait to get back to wearing clothes for me rather than him. There will still be the skater skirt and biker boots, but it will be my choice. Take it or leave it.'

'I understand,' said Cherry. 'Won't be long now. Just think what his reaction will be on Friday.'

'I will,' Anji said. 'It'll make it all worthwhile.'

I made coffee for everyone, and Cherry and I sat side by side at the conference table, me with the notes we had made the previous evening in the search of the office and Cherry with the laptop. She opened a new spreadsheet document and filled in the names for the columns: name of client; name of solicitor; bank account number; sort code. I then dictated while she typed them in.

Then came the clever part. We sorted the clients by alphabetical order and saved that. Then sorted by solicitor and saved that, then by bank account, ditto. We printed everything out and prepared the next to-do item for the day. Calling on Palmer.

He had on a different suit today — black with a thick silver pinstripe. It still didn't fit him. This was a man with no time to spare for trying on clothes. Or, perhaps, one with a wife who chose them for him and estimated his size wrongly.

'This better be worth it, Shannon. I've got other fish to fry.'

'I'm going to solve the case, but I don't want any action until Friday.'

'Can't promise anything,' he said.

'Then bugger off back to your other fish,' I said.

He snorted. 'Let's just say I'll hear your story and decide then.'

'Let's just say bugger off.'

'Gentlemen,' Cherry said. 'This doesn't have to be a boxing match. There doesn't have to be a winner and loser. We all need to work together. Let's start again. Good morning, Detective Inspector Palmer. How are you today?'

Palmer thought about it.

'I'm fine, thank you. And yourself, Ms Walker?'

'I'm well. Can I get you some coffee or tea?'

'Coffee would be good.'

'What sort of coffee would you like? We can do espresso, latte, whatever you want.'

'Espresso would be good.'

'Then excuse me, one moment.'

Cherry got up to relay the coffee orders to Morag.

'No fighting while I'm gone, boys,' she said.

'What shall we talk about while she's gone?' Palmer said.

'Cricket,' I said. 'It's a slow game, but you get a result in the end.'

Thankfully Cherry returned before too long. 'This is what we will do. Shannon will tell you the story. If you act before Friday, you won't find out the murderer and the accomplice. You'll also mess up an embezzlement case. We ask you to be patient, DI Palmer.'

Palmer nodded. The coffee arrived, and I set off to explain as much as I could.

'We're looking for two people,' I said. 'Two, not one. One person sets off the fire alarm while the other commits the murder. There will be an attempt at fraud on Friday — the last Friday of the month. The busiest day of the month for conveyancing. The fraudsters will try to divert money from the accompanying solicitors to an account or accounts that they have set up.'

'How do you know this?' said Palmer.

'Because they had a dry run a couple of Fridays ago,' I said. 'No one picked it up except a solicitor called Alan Jones, who complained about the delay in receiving his payment. That's why Ackroyd was killed. When we were tasked with valuing the practice, our culprits feared that we would spot something was wrong and they would have to abandon their plans. They hoped that his death would scupper the whole deal and cancel our contract, leaving them free to commit the fraud.'

'So who are our fraudsters, our murderers?' he asked.

'I know one of them for sure, Sarah Jenkins. Nothing can be paid out without her authorization. She was the one who set off the fire alarm. She's a smoker, so no one would think anything was wrong when they joined her outside, having a fag, when the alarm sounded. She set off the alarm, went outside, lit a cigarette.'

'And the other culprit?' he asked.

'I have some ideas from their trial run, but I'd like to see that proved beyond doubt. That's why we are waiting till Friday. Whoever is the other fraudster is also the murderer. He joins Ackroyd for the cake and Madeira ritual, eats his cake, drinks his Madeira, poisons Ackroyd, takes his own glass to make it look like a stroke or heart attack or even suicide, and goes out of the French doors as I showed you the other day, locking them. He waits until a few people have gathered. Jenkins, smoking all the time, walks to the back of the building, and he joins her. All very natural.'

'So what are you hoping I will do?' he said.

'Position yourself and other officers outside the building and wait for our culprits to come out. Cherry and I will be monitoring the transactions and cancelling them. When the fraudsters reckon they have enough money — or, for them the worse scenario — see that we are on to them, they will do a runner. We will be able to see when they are going to disappear, because we are watching everything and reversing all transactions so they don't go through. That's when we can give you the signal to jump in. Only then will we know who killed Ackroyd.'

'So why shouldn't I just arrest this Jenkins woman and sweat her?' he said.

'Good old-fashioned police tactics, eh? Because she will know she can just admit to a charge of fraud and stand a chance of getting a light sentence or even a suspended sentence and you'll never find out for sure who the murderer is.'

'If you forget your differences, DI Palmer,' said Cherry, 'you'll see this is the best route there is to catching the murderer. That's what we all want to know.'

'Any suspicions, Shannon?' he said.

'Plenty. I have a name from the dry run, but I don't have enough proof to make anything stick. Maybe a smoker, but I can't be sure of that. That would put Baker, Samson, Kirby and Seymour in the frame. Baker and Samson would lose out on the sale of their shares, though, but they will be aiming for more than that from the fraud. Average transactions, say, three hundred thousand. In the course of a couple of hours, they could switch five transactions, maybe more. One and a half million, minimum. Depends how much they are prepared to hang around; how greedy they are.'

'Okay, let me think,' Palmer said. 'In the meantime, more coffee would be good.'

My turn. I went to see Morag, leaving the office door slightly open so I could listen to what was going on.

'How much do you trust him to keep his word?' I heard Palmer say.

'Explicitly. He believes in honour. It would not be honourable to break his promise, to break any promise. He has his faults — boy, does he have his faults — but you can trust him.'

I rejoined Palmer and Cherry and was followed by Morag with more coffees. I sat back down and turned to Palmer. 'Have you come to a decision?' I asked.

'I like your coffee,' he said.

I leaned back in the chair and sighed.

'Two can play your game, Shannon,' he said. 'But I'll go along with you. What you said makes perfect sense. If it doesn't pan out on Friday, I'll arrest Jenkins and try and make something stick. That's all I can promise. Except, if you break your promise, I'll come down on you as hard as I can. Every time you are out driving, you'll be stopped and searched. I'll have the fire department all over the building and find some excuse to shut it down. Every trick I can play, I'll play it. Your life won't be worth living.'

'Sounds like a deal, then,' I said.

* * *

That evening, we sat together in our lounge waiting for Arthur to return from his evening vigil. He had been focussing on Jenkins again. It would be interesting to know if she had repeated the pattern from the previous night.

'Sorry I'm late,' he said, when he finally arrived back. 'Hard to keep pace with her lifestyle. Does she never take a break?'

'Tell us all about it while I get you a beer,' I said. I went over to the fridge, took out a bottle and popped the cap. I handed it to Arthur and he took a big swig straight out of the bottle.

'Nectar,' he said sighing.

'So?' said Cherry.

'Same system as last night. Everything repeated. Cab comes at eight. Dressed the same: short red leather skirt with the slit up the side.'

Cherry and Anji raised their eyebrows.

'What am I missing here?' I asked.

'You don't wear the same outfit two days running,' Anji said patiently. 'Shows you have a lack of imagination or a limited wardrobe and, therefore, strapped for cash.'

'She was gone for three and a half hours,' Arthur said. 'Might have gone somewhere after the meal or maybe skipped the meal entirely. And what about the bloke she's meeting? We're looking for someone who has stamina.'

'The big question is,' I said, 'where do we go from here? I don't think there's much point following Jenkins again. She's having an affair, for sure, but with whom? I need to think of what comes next. Let me sleep on it. Might be time to take a night off, Arthur.'

'That would be good,' he said, 'though I'd like to satisfy my curiosity on who the guy is.'

'I suspect all will be revealed in time,' I said.

'Patience is a virtue,' Norman said. 'Are we virtuous enough?'

The silence answered his question.

CHAPTER THIRTY-FOUR

'What's my motivation for this role?' Beryl said.

Since agreeing to be part of the scam against Jinx, she had gone all actressy on me.

We were standing in the sitting room of her Georgian house. With its portico-columned frontage, it screamed money. It almost had 'easy pickings' on a fluorescent sign on the wide front door. Inside, it featured large rooms with high ceilings and original features, such as ceiling roses and dado rails. Jinx would find it irresistible.

The sitting room had a polished wood floor, which was to be particularly useful during the sting as it would amplify the sound of footsteps. It was a large room, uncrowded by too much furniture. Two cats had commandeered a sofa and were fast asleep. Domesticity: all adds to the touch. The focal point of the room was a wood-burning stove with a sofa on each side, both covered in a chintzy print featuring peacocks. Between the two sofas, there was a wooden but-ler's table with a tea tray on top. The tray had a pot, two cups and saucers, a sugar bowl and a milk jug on it. It said cosy . . . and, with the willow pattern on each part of the set, wealth. Irresistible.

The most important article was placed on a small chest opposite the window, where the light would strike it, so it couldn't be missed — the Chinese vase.

'You're the mercenary one,' I said. 'You're the one looking for the big kill.'

'Am I dressed properly?' she said.

She was in what I assumed was her favourite twinset in cream with a pearl necklace, diamond ring and emerald brooch.

'You're dressed fine,' I replied, trying to keep the irritation from my voice.

'Only I wouldn't want to be underdressed.'

'No chance of that,' I said.

I checked my watch — fifteen minutes to go before Jinx was due to arrive. The tea was going to be stewed, but Jinx would have had far worse inside prison.

'I wish I had done some scones,' said Beryl, obviously fretting.

I couldn't suppress a sigh. 'Beryl,' I said, 'Jinx wouldn't be interested if the scones had currants and came with clotted cream and home-made jam.'

'Not even if it was strawberry jam?'

I couldn't suppress this sigh, either. 'Remember, Beryl, he has come with one purpose only — to rip you off. Just react at the appropriate time.'

The doorbell rang. He was early. And what did we hope he had been doing in the time since Nancy's visit? Googling Chinese vases. And seeing the ad on eBay that Anji had placed under the name of the fictitious Lee Ho — a man desperate for Chinese vases and saying he would pay ten grand for a matching pair.

Jinx would look at the picture he had taken of Nancy's vase and be rubbing his hands together. Here was a punter that was ripe for the skinning: a lady who would fall for his charm and be fleeced.

I retreated to the kitchen and listened, as before, from my position of a part-open door.

I heard Beryl welcome him, and the sounds of his shoes on the wooden floor. He had stepped into the sitting room, and then there was silence. He would be taken in completely by the prominent vase. The mental till would be going *Ker-ching!*

'Tea, Mr . . . ?' Beryl asked.

'That would be a kindness I hope I can repay later.'

Tea was poured, and there was some stirring in of sugar from Jinx — a three-spoonful man, as I remember — and an awkward silence.

'It's like this,' Beryl said. 'Times are hard. My widow's pension doesn't go as far as it used to. I need cash.'

'I understand,' said Jinx sympathetically. 'I've come across this situation before. You're not alone. Now, down to business — the tea's lovely, by the way. Such hospitality. The Chinese vase. Is this the one?'

There was silence while, I presumed, Beryl nodded.

'I'll give you five hundred for it.'

A sound of spluttering.

'Do excuse me,' said Beryl, 'but that is way off the mark. The value for one is at least a thousand. For two, I suppose ten thousand would be around the mark, if you can find the one to match. I would prefer to hang on for the larger sum, if we can find the missing vase of the pair.'

'Excuse me for a moment. Another cup of tea, perhaps, while I answer my messages. They could be important.'

There was silence again. Messages! Checking the photo of Nancy's vase.

'I could give you a thousand, I think.'

He would be thinking one thousand for Nancy's vase and one thousand for Beryl's would equal eight thousand profit when Lee Ho paid up.

'It doesn't sound like enough to me,' came the reply. 'I was thinking more like five.'

The profit equation was moving away from Jinx. Still money to be made, though.

'How about three? Jinx said. 'That would be a fair price. I did notice there's a little crack starting to spread around the base.'

'I'll tell you what,' said Beryl. 'We'll split the difference. We'll settle for four thousand. Cash, of course. Such a performance for us getting to a bank. So undignified, haggling.'

While Beryl hesitated, as per the script, to build the tension, Jinx would be remaking his calculations. Four grand for this vase would still see him double his money.

'Done,' he said. 'Let's shake on it.'

Count your fingers afterwards, I thought.

'It will take me a few days to get the cash. Can I take the vase in the meantime?'

'So sorry, but no,' Beryl said. 'I'll keep it until then.'

Damn, Jinx would be thinking. There had been a chance there where he could have taken the vase and done a disappearing act. They had a mobile number, and he could easily buy another phone, and they didn't know his name — he'd been careful not to tell them that.

'I'll be back in a couple of days, then.'

I heard his footsteps receding as he moved to the door.

Live by the sword, Jinx . . .

CHAPTER THIRTY-FIVE

Wednesday, and I had a call from Fiona. Could I go to her place for a talk? I wondered why she would want a meeting. We settled on eleven a.m. and I set off for the drive to Dulwich.

'I have cold feet,' she said, when we were in the sitting room with a pot of tea. Best tea set, too. 'Am I doing the right thing? Those poor members of the long-serving staff who will lose their jobs, their lives in the happy family.'

'You've got that extra quarter of a million for compensation. That would average out at around twelve grand per person. What's that? Around six months' salary, tax-free? I think that's a generous amount. You shouldn't fret about it.'

'What about poor Roger?' she said. 'Maybe I'm doing just what the murderer wants?'

'Probably not,' I said. 'I think the motive for the murder was to stop the takeover, or at least stall it. You're doing the opposite. I shouldn't feel bad about it. It's a good deal. I don't think you could have squeezed any more from Randall.'

'You know, don't you?' she said abruptly. 'You know who poisoned Roger?'

I had to be guarded here. I could not jeopardize the committing of the fraud. If that happened, we would never find out for sure who the murderer was.

'I have suspicions, but don't know for certain and at the moment, I don't have enough proof. Best to leave that to DI Palmer. I realize it must be difficult for you having Roger's killer still at large, but we will get him or her in the end. Please be patient. Now is not the time for action.'

'Do you think it was someone at the practice?' she persisted. 'An inside job, I suppose the police would call it?'

'Almost certainly,' I said. 'There were no visitors that afternoon. At least none spotted by Nancy. Makes it even harder to accept. A snake in the grass.'

'I miss him,' she said. 'He had his habits — always liked a pink gin when he arrived home. No one has had a pink gin since the days of the Raj. He liked to keep traditions. I respect him for that.'

'Everyone speaks highly of him,' I said gently. 'They laud him for being a gentleman of the old school. A dying breed, unfortunately. Although dying should not be like this.'

'And how should it be?'

'In fighting for a cause. In doing something honourable. Roger, when he retired, would have found something to fight for. He was that kind of man.'

'"Kind" is the right word to use for him. Never said a bad word against anyone,' she said.

'How are you coping with the admin side of his death — sorting out bank accounts and so on? If we can help, don't hesitate to call us. No fee.'

'Most of our money was in the stock market. His broker will sort that out. There's enough cash in the bank for a few months, but thanks for the offer. And, of course, there's the money from Randall to come.'

'If I were you, I would insist on payment being made the moment the contract is signed. I don't trust Randall and won't feel happy until the money is in the bank. He can afford it — we've seen his accounts: he has plenty of assets. Don't let him stall. You're doing the right thing. Remember that. Make him pay.'

'You don't like him, do you? Is your advice affected by that?'

'The more I know about him, the less I think of him, but be assured he will get his comeuppance.'

She nodded. 'Roger's funeral is set for Thursday next week. Will you come?'

'I will bring Anji, too. She met him, although only briefly. She thought highly of him, too. We will be honoured to come.'

'You are like Roger, you know? He valued honour a lot. Always stand by your word and keep your promises. That's what he used to say.'

CHAPTER THIRTY-SIX

'He's late,' said Cherry, unusually tense.

Anji, for whom this whole scam had been created, nodded in agreement. Keep cool, I thought.

It was early evening, and we were at Beryl's house awaiting the arrival of Jinx. The troops were out in force, everyone wanting to be in on the kill. Cherry, particularly, had a key role to play

'Relax,' I said to Anji. 'He'll come.'

'What if he can't raise the money?' she said. 'What if he senses that something is wrong? That it's all too coincidental?'

'Jinx is a shark. He can smell blood in the water. He won't be able to resist it.'

Anji looked away from me and took in Beryl's kitchen, as if to find something familiar to make her feel less uncomfortable. The room was dominated by a big Aga but I doubted that made her feel better. There was a range of cupboards and worktops in honey oak and a refectory table and two benches — no joy there.

'Hell,' Cherry said to Anji. 'We might as well sit down.'

Anji sat on one of the benches and drummed her fingers on the table.

I topped my coffee up from the pot on the Aga and sat down opposite her. I resisted the temptation to place my hand on hers, if only to stop her displacement activity.

'Where the hell is he?' Cherry said.

The doorbell jangled, and she jumped up and opened the kitchen door a fraction. I heard Beryl's footsteps as she crossed the floor of the sitting room, then Jinx's cheery voice. And didn't he have a lot to be cheery about? Five thousand reasons. Or so he thought.

'So good to see you again,' he said to Beryl.

'I've been looking forward to this,' Beryl said.

'Well,' Jinx said, 'I have your money, so time to complete the deal.' I could hear the rustling of a paper bag. 'No need to count it. You can trust me.'

I almost spluttered at the statement.

There was a silence while, as instructed, Beryl checked the cash anyway to make sure it wasn't phoney and that it added up to four thousand.

Satisfied, she said, 'Perhaps you would like to join us in a celebration.'

I pressed the number on my phone. Nancy should now have entered the front door. Beryl came into the kitchen, smiling from ear to ear. She handed over the money, and Anji relaxed.

Beryl took the bottle from the fridge and I opened it with a very satisfying pop. She put the bottle on a tray with six glasses and carried it carefully through to the sitting room.

'That's a lot of glasses,' Jinx said.

'One for each of us,' I said on entering.

Jinx staggered back. 'What the fuck are you doing here, Shannon?'

'Ladies present, Jinx,' I said. 'Moderate your language, please.'

Nancy stepped into the room.

Jinx looked at the glasses and added them up to four of us. Anji entered the room — make that five. Then Cherry entered.

'Let me introduce you to our final guest,' I said. 'Detective Chief Inspector Walker of the Fraud Squad.'

Cherry stepped out of the kitchen and flashed her phoney warrant card. I poured the champagne and handed the glasses around. 'You might as well have a drink, Jinx. It's all you're going to get today. Plus the vase, of course.'

'What the . . . hell is going on?'

'You made a big mistake,' I said. 'You scammed Anji's gran. Today you've learned a big lesson. Never trust an old lady or a wrathful granddaughter.'

'But I've still got the vases. I'm still five grand up. Aren't I?'

'You haven't got any smarter over the years, Jinx. There are no vases plural. Nancy's presence should have told you that. There's just one vase and that we picked up from a junk shop.'

'What about my four grand?'

'Thank you for that, Jinx. Consider us Robin Hood and his merry ladies. We're robbing the rich — that's you — to pay the poor — that's the likes of Anji's grandmother.'

'And we're very grateful,' said Anji.

'But . . .' Jinx stammered.

'No one forced you to buy the vase,' I said.

'What about Lee Ho? I can still get some money from him.'

'There is no Lee Ho.'

'But I saw the ad on the internet . . .'

'That's another lesson you've learnt today. Don't believe everything you see on the internet.'

Jinx's eyes roved around the room as if to find something that said this was unreal. Some cruel joke that we would all laugh at in a moment. No chance.

Cherry turned her beautiful eyes on him and said, 'We can play this two ways. Hard or soft. Soft involves you walking away a free man, only a little lighter in your wallet.'

'And hard?'

'I arrest you.'

'On what charge?'

'On whatever charge I want, and with your record you'll be going down for a long stretch.'

'But that's not legal,' he protested.

'Stop whining, Jinx,' she said. 'Accept the inevitable.'

'Anything else to add, Shannon?' Cherry asked.

I shook my head.

'Then you're free to go, Jinx,' Cherry said. 'An expensive lesson. I trust it will make you wiser. Just remember I'm on your case. Step out of line and you go straight to prison.'

He glared at me and stormed out of the house.

He never touched his champagne. How ungrateful can you get?

CHAPTER THIRTY-SEVEN

The funeral was a burial and was held at the church in Dulwich Village. It was a fine morning with dew sparkling on the grass from the hazy sunlight. There was a light breeze, and a chill in the air which would disappear when the sun rose higher in the sky. The ceremony started at ten a.m., and those in the know were wrapped up well, as the church was not heated. While not a small church, it was fully packed with those who wanted to pay their respects to Ackroyd and relive their memories of the man. The answerphone at the office had been switched on and the office closed — every one of the staff was present. The crowd was also swelled by people from the legal profession and — I thought unnecessarily so — by Randall.

Cherry, Anji and I were seated on uncomfortable pews and were relieved when we could stand up to sing a hymn. The music, played on a keyboard in organ mode, was sombre; I felt that it was probably not what Roger would have wanted — I was sure something more rousing was his style.

I was wearing the same black suit, white shirt and black tie that I had worn at Arlene's funeral. My mind was taken back to that sad day. I thought of the ten happy years we had spent with each other before cancer took its inevitable toll.

I did not wonder what she would have thought of Walker, always *Walker* not *Cherry* in those days, and I falling in love, and, hopefully, us spending our days together. Arlene would have wanted me to be happy, even though Cherry would have seemed an unlikely choice. Or maybe not: women have an inner radar that men do not have where love is sensed. Female intuition? I didn't know. Whatever it was, it seemed to work.

Both Cherry and Anji, naturally, were in black, although Anji had obviously eschewed the little black dress that so enthralled Randall. She wore a long black coat over a simple black skirt and white blouse with a black scarf. Cherry was wearing a black dress with a long black cardigan that reached the knee length of her dress.

The sermon was short, to make way for the number of people who wanted to pay a homily to Ackroyd. We filed out to the sound of *The Arrival of the Queen of Sheba* — more like it — following Fiona, her family and the coffin to the graveside and standing in a circle surrounding the grave. The vicar recited a prayer, and we all mumbled our amens at the end. Fiona had been stoic up until that part, but the tears flowed as the coffin was lowered into the grave. Someone had had the appropriate idea of bringing along a bottle of Madeira and that was laid on top of the coffin. With that, Ackroyd was at peace.

I looked around the group of solicitors that stood in the sunlight, thinking that two of them were being hypocrites. Still, justice would be done soon. I had to be patient.

There were trees in the churchyard providing shelter for those days when the rain came down. Under one tree was Arthur, and at another, Palmer.

I looked at Arthur.

He nodded back.

I looked at Palmer.

He didn't.

CHAPTER THIRTY-EIGHT

Friday morning: the mood was sombre, and the signing was scheduled for nine a.m. Be good to get it out of the way, so we could concentrate on other things. Cherry and I had the laptop set up on the table together with the printouts of the spreadsheets. If the trial run was evidence, we knew who we should be watchful of. We were concentrating on the transactions at the same time as running the meeting — although, if we were right, nothing would happen for a while.

Fiona, Baker and Samson sat on one side of the table; Cherry, Anji and I on the other side, and Randall at the head again. Anji was wearing her business look to mirror Cherry — played down, no flashing of leg or bosom today, no cheap thrills for Randall. The contract of sale was placed on the table in front of Fiona. Signatures were required from everybody unless Fiona used her majority shares to override the two other partners. Cherry and I would act as witnesses.

'I take it no one has had a change of heart?' I asked.

'When do I get the money?' asked Samson.

'Same question from me,' said Baker.

'Right now,' said Randall. 'Just give me your bank details and I'll send the money across.'

Samson wrote on his notepad, tore off the page and slid it across to Randall. Fiona and Baker did the same.

'Sign the contract and I'll give my authorization to my PA. We, as a sound business,' he bragged, 'have plenty of assets on our balance sheet and our bank has been informed. You should have the money within the hour. Let's get this over and done with.'

Fiona signed the document and passed it to Baker. He did the same, and then it was time for Samson. He scribbled a signature and handed it to Randall. He signed and gave it to Cherry, who signed, and I added my signature as the second witness. For some reason, Anji declined to sign. That wasn't necessary, though.

Randall took out his phone and made the important call. 'All done,' he said. 'Time to go.'

'Not yet,' I said to Randall. 'We have some other business for you.'

The others left the room. Anji took a document from her new briefcase. She passed it to Randall. 'This is a transcript of interviews I have had with your female staff. You'd better read it.'

Randall began to frown as he read: the more he read, the deeper the frown.

'What is this about?' he said.

'We have enough material here to take you to an employment tribunal,' I said. 'Your behaviour is way out of normal standards. We're going to give you the opportunity to have a clean sheet. To change your ways. If you don't agree, we'll start to take legal proceedings. Your reputation will be trashed forever, and you'll be giving lots of money in recompense to employees past and present. Should be an easy decision. What do you say?'

'These accusations wouldn't stand up in court. Did you tell them they were being recorded?'

'Your treatment of me will be enough,' Anji said. 'The rest will be taken as corroboration. A trip to Paris will be sufficient to finish you. Would you have made such an arrangement for a male employee?'

Randall suddenly looked resigned. 'What is it you want me to do?'

'We have prepared an email to all staff,' Anji said. 'You will inform them of the takeover of Ackroyds and say that you have taken the opportunity to review dress codes. All employees will wear smart clothes, as if there were client meetings that day. There is no need to wear shoes with heels and all skirts should not of necessity be short. Oh, by the way, Paris is out for you.'

'But I've paid for the air fare and the hotel,' he blustered.

'They won't be wasted,' Anji said. 'Your wife has been told that this was meant to be a surprise for her. She'll be waiting for you at Heathrow.'

'You've stitched me up,' he said angrily.

'No. We've given you the opportunity to unstitch yourself,' I said. 'What do you say now?'

'You seem to have covered everything,' he said.

'Oh, not everything,' I said. 'There's more to come. In the meantime, Anji will send the appropriate email for you to copy and paste. That . . .'

Cherry interrupted: 'Game on.'

I looked at the screen. Amount authorized to a different account than it should have been.

'Three hundred thousand,' Cherry said.

'Blocked,' I said. 'How many times do you think it will take before they realize that no money has been sent?'

'Three,' said Cherry. 'There will be other transactions going through. At one, they will be thinking it's a glitch. Two will seem like coincidence. Three will tell them something is going very wrong.'

In the end, it was four, not three, although I would have agreed with her. Signs that they are desperate.

'And another,' Cherry said. 'Four hundred thousand.'

'You'd better watch us saving you money,' I said to Randall.

He moved over to watch Cherry.

'Five hundred thousand,' she said.

I blanked the transaction, then made the phone call. 'Any minute now.'

'Another five hundred thousand,' she said, taking the invoice and filling in the blanks. She handed it to Randall.

'What's this?' he said.

'Time to re-read our contract with Ackroyds. Ten per cent of any frauds discovered. Money saved: one point seven million. Ten per cent as agreed: one hundred and seventy thousand. As the proud owner of Ackroyds, you are now liable to pay us this amount. I did cover that at our briefing meeting and it's there in black and white in the small print.'

'But no one reads the small print,' he said lamely.

'So you didn't read the clause about giving up your youngest grandson to be apprenticed to a chimney sweep?' I quipped. 'That was Anji's idea, by the way. We all had a chuckle about that.'

'But a hundred and seventy thousand! I never thought it would come to that.'

'What is it they say? Ignorance is no defence in law.'

'But . . .' he began to say.

'And,' I said, 'as you said earlier, as a sound business you have plenty of assets. We've seen your accounts, too, as part of our valuation of the practice; we know you can afford it. So, be a good boy and pay us our due.'

'But,' he spluttered again.

'No more buts,' I said. 'We still have access to your bank. We can do it ourselves, if you like, but for such a large amount, I would prefer you to authorize the payment. Remember what you are making from the takeover. With synergy, you'll still be making a handsome profit. Cherry will accompany you back to your office to oversee the payment.'

'No more transactions going through,' Cherry said. 'They've made a runner.'

Jenkins and Samson.

Right into the arms of DI Palmer.

I was right.

But wait. Too quick, Shannon. Be careful of hubris — the sin of pride.

Jenkins and Samson were followed hot on their heels by Baker and Seymour.

I was wrong. Damn. She was cleverer than I had thought.

I had missed the vital clue. The same outfit two days running. It was different men.

CHAPTER THIRTY-NINE

Sarah Jenkins was obvious, of course. Nothing went in or out of the bank without her authorization. Her partner in crime — one of her partners in crime, we now knew — was, again, not unexpected because of the dry run — Samson. He of the tinted glasses that hid his nil eye contact. He of the boring marriage, judging by the photo buried in a desk drawer, and dreams of a life in the sun. They were handcuffed and in the back of one of the police cars. Baker and Seymour followed behind in separate cars. I called Cherry and gave her a task.

'Would you like to sit in, Shannon?' said Palmer. 'Be good to have an expert on fraud.'

'I'd be delighted,' I said. 'See the job through to the end.'

'I don't know enough at the moment to charge them with murder, so we'll start with the frauds. Are you sure of your facts?'

'Without a doubt.'

'Then let's get to it.'

We travelled the short distance to the police station, and all the culprits were put in separate cells. No chance of them speaking together and trying to put forward an alternative universe to explain their actions.

'Who shall we start with?' Palmer asked.

'There's more evidence against Jenkins, so best to start with her,' I said. 'Plus the fact she's a smoker. She'll be thinking of when she can have the next fag. Be more vulnerable.'

Palmer led me along a corridor and into a large windowless room fitted with a one-way mirror, so that proceedings could be watched by more people than the two sat in chairs on one side of a long table.

Jenkins was led in still handcuffed — for effect, I thought, rather than security. As habit had it, Jenkins was a chameleon against the magnolia walls of the room.

'Poking your nose in here, too, Shannon?' she snapped. 'Do you never stop?'

Palmer ignored her and went through the normal litany of the caution and the recording of the interview. Told her she could call a lawyer, which she declined. 'I have done nothing wrong,' she said, 'so why should I need a lawyer?'

'Shannon tells me you've been a naughty girl dipping your hands in the till. Do you deny this?'

'I don't have to deny anything,' she said. 'It's your job to prove it.'

'Tell me about your day at work today,' Palmer persisted.

'Normal day,' she said. 'Lots of activity, as it was the last Friday in the month — conveyancing going manic. I just did my job, processing the transactions. Why? Was something wrong?'

'During the course of the morning,' I said, 'you moved transactions from the client account to three new fraudulent accounts which I suspect were set up by you and your accomplices. We know all this because of your failed attempts this afternoon. You were going to use that money to ride off into the sunset. Start a new life together, maybe, with whichever one you chose, or even go solo.'

She didn't flinch. 'I was very busy,' she said. 'If some of the transactions were fraudulent, I didn't notice them. Just took them at face value. How was I supposed to know?'

'The maxim is "follow the money",' I said. 'What would we find if we did that?'

I passed Palmer a note.

'Tell me about your relationship with Samson,' he said.

She shrugged. 'Just a working relationship. We are colleagues, nothing else. Your turn, Mr Plod.'

I sighed inwardly. She was a cool customer. I doubted we could get much that was incriminating.

My phone beeped. It was a short text — just two words, more to follow. Cherry had worked miracles.

'Tell me about an account called Paradise Regained Limited?' I said.

'I need a lawyer,' she replied.

That was all we were going to get out of her.

* * *

Next up was Samson. He was less assured than Jenkins. Twitchy. Playing with the bezel of his chronometer watch. He was scared, that much was obvious. The original plan was to drain as much as possible from the client account and disappear. He hadn't factored this in. He was going to brazen it out. At the back of his mind now was the fact that we had previously interviewed Jenkins.

'Tell me about your relationship with Sarah Jenkins?' Palmer asked. 'Are you more than just colleagues?'

'I don't understand your interest.'

I passed Palmer another note.

'On Wednesday last week, you sent a taxi for Jenkins and had a nice dinner together.'

We were flying by the seat of our pants here. He didn't know it was Arthur who gave us the information, and that we didn't know which one of the three of them had been her dinner date that evening. It was a lucky guess. The only rationale was that Jenkins had told us.

'It was just a meeting of friends, nothing more, nothing less. So hard to find time for conversation during the working day.'

'So what did you converse about at dinner? Business or social?' Palmer said.

'Just chit-chat, you know? She has a dog that needs walking at inconvenient times of the day — crack of dawn and sunset just when she wants to enjoy the end of the working day. She tries to be vegetarian, but can't resist a bacon sandwich. You know, that kind of thing.'

'And what did she eat that evening?' Palmer asked. 'Among the small talk.'

'She had lobster to start, and Dover sole as her main.'

'Sounds expensive,' Palmer said.

'Well, Martine's is a classy joint. You expect to pay for quality.'

Well done, Palmer. We now knew exactly where they went. Gold dust when we next spoke to Jenkins.

'And tell us all about Newlife?' Palmer asked.

'I think I need to speak to a lawyer,' he answered.

'Should be spoilt for choice,' I said.

And that was all we were going to get out of him, too, for the moment.

* * *

Baker looked bemused. As well he might. He'd expected to make a hasty retreat into the sunset with Jenkins, and here he was in the cells along with Samson and Seymour. His world was about to fall apart.

'Going on holiday?' Palmer said. He slid a plane ticket across to Baker which they had found in the routine search of the cars; a constable had brought it in and handed it to Palmer. 'Packed suitcase in the car? Jetting away to distant parts? I suppose Orlando is nice at this time of year.'

'Bit of sun does wonders any time of year, especially when you've just lost your job,' Baker muttered.

'Single ticket, not return,' Palmer said.

'Didn't know how long I would stay.'

'Going on your own, Mr Baker?'

'No one to go with,' Baker said.

'I'm inclined to believe you,' Palmer said. He slid another ticket across the table. 'It seems Ms Jenkins had the same idea. Except she's off to Athens.'

Baker's face fell. He stared at the ticket. Was this possible, or was Palmer playing a trick?

'Seems like you've been dumped, Mr Baker. Big time, one might say.'

'I want to talk to a lawyer,' Baker said.

'Well, aren't you lucky,' said Palmer. 'We happen to have one doing the okey cokey in the cells at this very moment. Henderson, is it? Shabby man. Five o'clock shadow? Grubby clothes?'

Baker nodded.

I passed my phone to Palmer. He read the message.

'Time for a break,' he said. Then, when we were outside, 'What do you think Ms Walker wants?'

'It said urgent,' I said. 'Only one way to find out.'

We walked to Palmer's office, where we could get some peace and quiet. Once seated, I dialled Cherry. 'You'll going to need a pad and pen,' she said.

'Ready,' I said, taking a notebook out of my pocket.

I listened intently. It was complex. I made a diagram on my pad and thanked her.

I showed the diagram to Palmer. 'This is how it works. There are three companies and three bank accounts set up ready to take the money from the fraud. Jenkins is a signatory on each one. The other signatories are: Newlife 1, Samson; Newlife 2, Baker; Newlife 3, Carlton Seymour. And then, this is what is interesting. All three accounts are to be closed today and all monies transferred to a new account named Paradise Regained. Sole signatory . . .'

'Don't tell me,' Palmer said. 'Sarah Jenkins!'

'She was going to double-cross all of them,' I said.

'Time to tell Baker the bad news,' Palmer said.

'And then Jenkins, Samson and Seymour.'

'All in good time, Shannon.'

We walked back to the interview room where Henderson was in deep conversation with Baker. Palmer restarted the recording equipment. 'Now where shall we go from here?' he said. 'I have enough evidence to charge you with fraud. That's small time when compared with murder. Tell me about the death of Roger Ackroyd?'

'My client would like to cut a deal,' Henderson interjected.

'Everyone always wants to cut a deal,' Palmer said. 'Tell me something new. Okay, tell me want you want?'

'My client will plead guilty to fraud, but wants not to be in the frame for anything to do with Ackroyd's murder.'

'You'll have to do better than that,' Palmer said. 'I don't take prisoners. Nor does Jenkins. She was going to dump the three of you and had all the money ready to go to a new account in her name. She swindled you all. So, tell me all about it?'

Henderson looked at Baker. 'I don't think you have an option,' he said.

'Where did the plan form?' Palmer asked. 'How did you start to get into this mess?'

'Sarah suggested we go out together for a meal,' Baker said. 'Catch up with things outside the office. She had even booked a restaurant. Seemed ungrateful to refuse. She was dressed to kill in a red leather skirt with a slit up the side. So different to the woman I knew from the office. I suppose you would say she got amorous. Touching my hand, you know? Playing footsie under the table. We went back to my place, and you can guess the rest.'

'And then you had pillow talk?' Palmer said.

'She said, wouldn't it be wonderful if we could go somewhere hot and sunny to spend the rest of our lives together? It sounded perfect,' Baker said. 'Then she told me how it could be done. Last Friday in the month, false account, getaway as soon as we had got enough. And then Shannon shows up.' He glanced at me. 'He'd been poking around and might have spotted something, could spoil everything. She just said she would handle it, and not to worry. She would make sure the deal with Randalls would be called off. Stick to the plan. I signed all the papers for the setting up of an off-the-shelf company and a bank account. I should have examined the papers more thoroughly, I suppose, but she was standing over me when I was reading, and I didn't want her to think I didn't trust her.'

'No one reads the small print,' I said. 'Hoisted on your own petard. How much were you aiming to get?'

'Sarah reckoned all we needed was two hours and we should get five million. She said she had done a pilot run and we would have plenty of time. She'd tell me when I needed to go, and we would meet at Heathrow. Split the money, fifty-fifty, book a hotel for a couple of nights while we looked for a property to buy. All beyond your wildest dreams.'

'Hook, line and sinker,' Palmer said. 'Didn't it ever occur to you that it all sounded too good to be true?'

'I was infatuated,' Baker said, shaking his head. 'Flattered, too, I suppose. I've been a fool, haven't I?'

'Where were you when the fire alarm went off?' Palmer asked, ignoring his question.

'Sat in my office working. I thought it was a false alarm. It's always a false alarm, isn't it?'

'Not much point having one, if that's the case,' I said.

'Did you see Jenkins, Samson or Seymour?' Palmer asked.

'Sarah wasn't in her office. Nor was Samson. Seymour passed me on the way out. When I got outside, Sarah was already there, smoking, as she always seems to be. Got me hooked on cigarettes again. Filthy habit. We said we'd stop when we got to America.'

'You fell for that one, too,' I said.

'Take him away, constable,' Palmer said. 'Make sure he doesn't get a chance to talk to any of the other prisoners. When he's safely locked up, bring in Seymour.'

Baker was led away.

'You've got enough evidence of the fraud, but four people who could have murdered Ackroyd,' I said. 'You need a breakthrough.'

Palmer frowned. 'Let's see what Seymour has to say.'

* * *

Seymour sat down, stared at Palmer defiantly and rubbed the scar on his left cheek as if reminding himself of harder times that had strengthened him mentally — what doesn't kill me makes me stronger. Nietzsche. Smart guy.

Seymour didn't look rattled. He was going to be a hard nut to crack.

'You've been double-crossed by Jenkins,' Palmer said. 'Show him your diagram, Shannon.'

'You weren't the only one to be deceived,' I said. 'If that makes you feel better. Although I doubt that from where you're sitting.' I showed him the diagram. 'Three companies set up — one for Baker, one for Samson and one for you — three bank accounts to receive the money. Then the switch. All three bank accounts to be drained, bled dry, and it all goes in an account in Jenkins's name. Result? Not a penny for you. You've been taken for a fool.'

'We've got enough to charge you with fraud,' Palmer said. 'Five years if you're lucky, given the size of it. But what about murder? Prison for life. Time to tell us all about it.'

'I had nothing to do with Ackroyd's murder,' Seymour said. 'You can't pin that on me. I must have a dozen witnesses who saw me leave my office after the fire alarm sounded and go straight outside. I wasn't anywhere near Ackroyd's office.'

'You see,' Palmer said, 'my problem is that because of the alarm and the confusion it caused, no one can remember for sure who was where. Even the receptionist can't say who went out at what stage. There's not one person who could testify honestly about what took place.'

'The murder was to get the merger stopped and me out of the picture,' I said.

'So,' Palmer said, 'the murder was linked to the fraud. I could have you as an accessory. Anything you'd like to say in your defence?'

'It all started innocent,' he said. 'She said we should have dinner together. She arrived at the restaurant . . .'

'. . . dressed in a red leather skirt with a slit up the side?'

'How did you know that?' Seymour said.

'You'd be surprised what we know,' Palmer said. 'Carry on.'

'We had too much wine. Went back to her house. You can guess the rest.'

'And she floated the idea about fraud?' Palmer said. 'Enough money to lose yourself for the rest of your lives?'

'I thought we could get a place in Jamaica. Sun and sand and golden rum. I even went on the internet to look for places for sale. It all seemed so easy. I couldn't resist it. Freedom from the machine that was going to control my life. The worm turns. End of story.'

'And how about the wife and kids?' I asked.

'End of story.'

'Take him away,' said Palmer to the constable on the door.

We sat there for a while. Palmer tidied his notes. 'This is getting messy,' he said.

'I don't see Baker as being a murderer,' I said. 'Just a silly lonely old man who got flattered by a younger woman.'

'In a red leather skirt with a slit up the side — good guess, Shannon. Baker didn't stand a chance, I agree with you. Too many morals, too lily-livered and not enough steel to commit a murder. Where do we go from here?'

'Time to dwell in their secret lives,' I said. 'We need search warrants.'

'Let's go for it,' he said.

* * *

It was time to change tack. Concentrate on the murder. Jenkins was brought back in with her lawyer.

'So,' Palmer said, 'tell us about the fire alarm? Whose idea was that?'

'No comment,' she said. Harrison smiled. Easy money for a series of "no comments".

'The murder of Roger Ackroyd needed a period of confusion,' Palmer said. 'The fire alarm was important in creating a scene where no one was quite sure who was where at the time. Whose idea was that?'

I could tell what was going through her mind. If Samson had squealed, should she admit what she had done? Turn Queen's evidence, in return for a lesser sentence?

'All I did was set off the fire alarm. What happened after that was none of my concern. Seemed like a bit of harmless fun to liven up a boring day. It's what lawyers do.'

'Your harmless fun is enough to make you an accessory before the fact for murder,' Palmer said.

'My client has no comment,' said her lawyer. 'You may as well discontinue the interview now.'

Palmer ignored him. 'Which takes us back a week or two to the start of the fraud, when, Mr Shannon tells me, you had a trial run. Did you deem it successful?'

'No comment.'

'You had dinner with Samson a week or two back. Lobster and Dover sole. I expect you remember that. Swanky place, Martine's; swanky prices to go with it.'

She hesitated. 'I'd like to talk to my lawyer in private.'

'Switch the recording system off,' the lawyer said. 'And the camera behind the mirror, just in case we have any lip readers.'

Palmer paused the equipment, and we went into the room behind the mirror.

'You need to chase up the search warrants for all of them,' I said.

'And what are we hoping to find?'

'Weedkiller,' I said. 'Weedkiller contains strychnine. Easy enough to boil it down and get a concentrated solution. Enough to poison Ackroyd.'

'Anything else?'

'Search for hard evidence of pre-planning, anything to connect them to Newlife — laptop, papers, go through their bins. The missing glass would be good, too, but that seems unlikely. The killer would have disposed of it by now. Cherry tells me Newlife and its variants must be newly formed companies — no need to file anything on record at Companies House as yet. Paradise Regained was the same. She's trying to pull a favour from her old friends in the Fraud Squad to trace the bank accounts for hard evidence on signatures. We just need to find a link, then it will all fall into place.'

'I'll get it organized,' Palmer said. 'Might even pop over to Samson's place myself if I get a moment. Join in the fun.'

Harrison made a signal at the mirror. They had finished their private conversation. We rejoined them.

'My client,' Harrison said, 'would like to cut a deal. She will admit to fraud if you drop the murder charge. All she did was set off the fire alarm. Whatever occurred after that is none of her doing.'

'And what about Paradise Regained?' I asked. 'Is that where the money trail ends?'

'I have enough to charge you with fraud,' said Palmer, 'without cutting any deal. From the fraud, I can link to murder. No deals. Interview suspended.'

He gathered up his papers, stopped the recording and we exited, leaving a uniformed constable to take Jenkins back to the cell where she could twitch from nicotine deprivation.

'Let's get a cup of coffee and take stock of progress,' he said.

He led me up a flight of stairs to the canteen, where the windows were steamed up by the boiling of giant urns of tea and coffee. Which was stewed and bitter. Just like our suspects, I thought, with the delight of irony.

'What next?' I asked. 'Will you cut her a deal?'

He shook his head. 'I don't like cutting deals when there's the chance of a conviction. I think we need to chase up those search warrants. Let's start with Samson. Tally ho.'

CHAPTER FORTY

Samson's place was a detached five-bedroom house in the leafy suburb of Hampstead. Good neighbourhood, low crime rate, decent schools, as much fresh air as you can get in London. I wondered whether he had a big mortgage dragging him down like lead weights on a diver.

His wife opened the door. She was a plain woman just the wrong side of thirty swathed in baggy clothes. There didn't seem much difference between her and Jenkins in her office persona. Samson didn't seem to learn from his mistakes. Mrs Samson — Iris, she told us — wore no make-up, and her black hair was gathered up in a badly done ponytail. She was wearing grey baggy tracksuit bottoms and a black loose sweater. She clutched at her face with both hands and started crying as we entered, fearing bad news. At least there was no mascara to run.

Palmer introduced us, the two SOCOs in their white suits and a female uniformed officer — mostly there for company, if needed — and explained why we were there. Iris didn't take it well. There was more to come, too, when she learnt about Jenkins. I thought she was well shot of him. At least, unless Samson had hidden it away somewhere, she had the money from the share sale to fall back upon while her husband was locked up in prison.

Iris took us into a sitting room that had children's toys scattered about — five bedrooms and no playroom. What's the point?

The sitting room had a three-piece suite in dark brown, practical with children if not pleasing to the eye. There were light-coloured curtains with dark tie-backs and a coffee table with books to make a statement — *A Brief History of Time* and other works supposed to paint the owners as intellectually superior.

The garden had a large lawn and a shed. We took one of the SOCOs and started there. It was filled with rusty tools and a petrol lawnmower that looked like it had seen better days. And there hidden behind some seedlings was the weedkiller. How predictable the criminal mind can be. Why not just ditch it? While the SOCO bagged it up and did a thorough search, Palmer and I went back inside.

'Does your husband have a study?' Palmer asked Iris.

'Upstairs,' she said. 'He doesn't like me and the kids going in there. Second door on the right. Try not to make a mess.'

Palmer, make a mess? God forbid. She didn't know him like I did.

The study was the size of a guest bedroom and, I suspected, had been earmarked in advance of the children coming along. There was a desk in one corner with a laptop on it and a pile of papers on the right-hand side. I riffled through them. Bills, unpaid, mainly. Where was the money going? Then I saw a receipt from a private school. It was all going on school fees: thousands each for three children every new term. That was the first thing that Iris would need to economize on. Added to a sky-high mortgage and his salary was sucked away each month.

Finished with the pile of papers, I put them back on the desk. Palmer picked them up and tapped them on the table so that there was no overlap between the pages and set them in the middle of the desk. He sighed, all back nicely in order.

I switched on the laptop. It was password-protected. I knew a man from Mid Anglia police force who could sort that out. Canning. Computer whizz. Handled the whole net-work for Mid Anglia police force. He could do things that even the smartest person at the Met would love to do. He owed me a favour. I called him and gave him the address of the police station and asked to come as soon as he was free. He said he was working on an urgent job and would be with me at six.

I checked a red filing cabinet along one wall and found stuff going back years — the house purchase of ten years ago, an unfinished manuscript of a novel with a rejection letter of three years in the past, old bank and credit card statements — running on overdraft and credit cards maxed out. Nothing linked to the fraud or the murder.

We left the SOCOs to do their job and went to join another team at Jenkins's house. Her house was a two-up two-down terrace in an area ripe for development if they could only raise the image of the locale. SOCO had gained entry and were looking especially for papers, bank statements and anything that was a record of the setting up of the company where the funds were supposed to go and stay. More weedkiller would be a bonus. The glass, too. Although that seemed unlikely.

The living room was small and had a modern sofa and a tan leather rocking chair in front of the TV. There was a bureau squeezed in front of one of the windows in the small living room where you could look out over the garden while tapping away. The bureau wasn't locked. It contained sta-tionery, envelopes, a diary and a notepad. The notepad was blank, but maybe could yield something when you did that trick with a pencil. The diary contained routine appoint-ments — doctor, dentist, that kind of thing — but nothing from this day on. A new life dawned.

There was a laptop on the kitchen table. I powered it up. No password needed. Everything was neatly packed away in descriptive folders. I looked first at a file that said 'bank statements'. There was money in the bank — not much, but, unlike Samson, she wasn't under any financial pressure. Her motive was pure greed.

There was no folder marked *Paradise Regained* or anything like it. This was going to take time. As an afterthought, I opened the recycle bin. And there it was. Paradise Regained.

The recycle folder held files such as instructions to the bank to set up an account, scans of passport and driving licence and council tax to support the application and transferring the sum of one thousand pounds as an opening balance.

'Have we got enough?' Palmer asked.

'More than enough,' I said.

'Let's take the laptop and head back,' he said.

'Give me a minute to go upstairs and look in her bedroom.'

'For what?'

'For curiosity's sake.'

I headed upstairs and into her bedroom. There was a large built-in wardrobe. I opened the doors. On one side, there were her dowdy work clothes; on the other, her clothes for outside of work. Dresses and short skirts, little black dresses, many pairs of shoes and boots with stiletto heels. Evidence of a whole new person. There on the rail was the red leather skirt with the split up the side. She hadn't packed it with the rest of the clothes she was taking with her. It had served its purpose.

'Our accountant has another side,' Palmer said. 'It's that side we need to prey on. Come on, Shannon. Let's press on and, hopefully, find something on Samson's laptop after your man has worked his magic.'

Laden with another laptop, we headed onwards.

* * *

Baker's mansion flat was like something from the 1920s. All it needed was a Jeeves. There was a large sitting room with two chesterfields and an antique trunk that was being used as a coffee table. A dining area was set to one side with a shiny yew table and four chairs of the same rich wood. The kitchen had old-fashioned oak cabinets and matching work-top and a small round table with two chairs for when he had a guest, which I doubted was often. There were no spare sherry glasses like the type used for Madeira. I checked the fridge and freezer — always a good place to hide something — and found them packed with ready meals. His bedroom had a king-size double bed with black sheets and duvet — prepared for spicy liaisons that would never take place. The whole arrangement seemed sad.

On the dining table was a laptop which we powered up and was not protected by a password — it was like he felt that he had nothing to hide. How wrong was he going to be? We briefly examined it. Outside of some dating sites, there were emails aplenty with Jenkins about details of the plan for a fraud, and plenty to connect him to Newlife. All enough to charge him for fraud, but no hard evidence for murder. We took the laptop and headed for the next on the list. Seymour.

* * *

Seymour's house was an ordinary three-bedroom semi in an ordinary suburb. There was no show of wealth here. It was a place handy for commuting, little else. I wondered what had brought him there. Maybe the schools were good: I didn't know. Seemed a poor choice for a well-off lawyer. Or maybe *poor* was the right word.

His wife opened the door. She was called Petal, and her face was lined with marks of stress. She was a large lady and was wearing a long, generous floral-print dress and a head wrap, only partly hiding the grey strands in her hair. I suspected from her dress she was as proud of her heritage as her husband.

She was puzzled at the sight of us — was Carlton in an accident and in hospital somewhere? Was he dead?

She led us through to the lounge. As we followed her, I could see into the kitchen where three children sat at a table having their tea. They were squabbling over a ketchup bottle; the noise level was high. The table was a mess. This could easily develop into a food fight. I bet that Petal couldn't wait for bedtime, or at least for Carlton to get home to share the load. Working late at Randalls might have suited him. I was beginning to see why the fraud, coupled with Jenkins, seemed attractive.

She reacted badly to the news that Carlton was in a cell at the police station — tell me something that wasn't obvious. We revealed no more than he was being held for fraud. Carlton could tell her the rest when they next met. If she reacted badly to fraud, what would she make of suspicion of murder and the affair with Jenkins?

The lounge was a narrow room like a railway carriage and was decorated in bright yellow emulsion on three walls and papered on the remaining wall with a pattern of leaves rising up out of a light green background. Along one long wall was a gas fire with a large Turkish rug in front of it. There was a three-piece suite in light-brown leather and everything looked neat and tidy. A haven away from the children.

We asked to see the rooms in the house, especially where he might have worked. Petal took us on a tour and there was a desk set up on the first-floor landing: didn't warrant a room to itself. On the top there was a laptop that was not password-protected — when will people learn to protect themselves? I pulled out the desk drawers while waiting for it to power up. In the bottom drawer was an up-to-date copy of the *Sporting Life* and a thick handbook on racing — all the results and form from last season. A picture, hardly surprising, was beginning to take shape in my mind.

The laptop revealed a frequent file labelled *bank* and I selected that. According to a spreadsheet, there was barely anything in the current account. Unless he had another file with a savings account, they were strapped for cash. Scrolling down the spreadsheet, all became clear. The name of an online betting firm kept coming up, mostly debits, but with the occasional credit to keep him hooked. He was an addict and had entered that phase where he was increasing his bets to try to make up his losses. He was reduced to going for the big kill.

I assumed his wife didn't know of his habit: she might be economizing on the housekeeping, scrimping and saving, while he was lining the bookies' pockets. He was up to his neck in it. Surely, she would go spare if she found out.

The spreadsheet of his bank account showed a large sum to British Airways for what must have been the flights for Jenkins and himself to Jamaica. The evidence was building up.

I checked the list of spreadsheets, but nothing else stood out, and went into his email account. Sure enough, there were incriminating exchanges with Jenkins, both regarding his affair and the plans for the fraud — details of hotel booked and plans for a swift getaway. Palmer rubbed his hands together and gave a rare smile — he had plenty of evidence to charge Seymour for fraud, and to put pressure on him to see if he could fit the bill for the murder.

We were almost there.

* * *

Canning was waiting for us. He had put on a bit of weight since I had last seen him. It suited him; he had looked gaunt in the past, weighed down by worries of everything that was happening in his life. I asked about his wife's health, hoping she was in a remission phase of her MS, and how his job was going.

'Life couldn't be better,' he said smiling. 'I owe you one.'

'Which you're just about to repay,' I said. 'We have a laptop which is password-protected and we need to investigate what's on it. This is DI Palmer — he's in charge of the case. You'll get on great with him. He likes to line up pencils, too.'

Palmer shook Canning's hand and took us to the interview room. We set up the laptop and waited while Canning did some esoteric things to it. Lines of green code came up on the black screen and he tapped away.

'What are you looking for?' he asked.

'Anything related to Newlife,' I said.

He tapped away again. 'Like this?'

Files from a search filled the screen. If there wasn't something incriminating here, I'm a Dutchman.

'Let's go from the top,' I said.

'I'd recommend doing it by date, starting with the earliest,' he said. 'More logical. Build a better picture bit by bit. Or byte by byte — that's a computer joke.'

Palmer and I craned our necks over Canning's shoulder as he called up the files. The oldest was just two months past. Letters to the bank setting up the account. So it had been a recent opening of the account. Seems like they hadn't thought long about what they needed to commit the fraud.

We progressed on to an email sent to Jenkins giving her details of the flight to Barbados where they hoped to reside in freedom, peace and luxury. A hotel confirmation was added as a download. There was an email from Jenkins regarding the trial run. She estimated, being safe, two hours before anyone would raise a fuss. Suitcases had to be kept to a minimum weight to speed through the rigmarole at the airport. They could buy what they needed when they arrived; markets there were filled to the brim with cheap clothes.

Seemed he'd been thinking of taking the hundred grand from the share sale, too. I hadn't liked him when we first met, and the more I learnt of him, the less I liked him. I hoped he would go down for a long time. Prison would break him. He would never be the same again. Take that from someone who had experienced it. It's some kind of hell.

CHAPTER FORTY-ONE

Then Palmer got the phone call. It was a member of the SOCO team at Samson's house. 'You better get over here,' he said.

Our hearts were beating with anticipation as we drove. They must have found something.

When we arrived, the SOCO took us into the kitchen. It was a large kitchen/diner with a big oak-topped island where you could watch and talk to the person doing the cooking. Along one wall was a dresser with glass panes for viewing the proudly displayed contents. The SOCO went over to the dresser and stood proudly in front of it.

'There was something at the briefing about a glass,' he said. 'Would this be it?'

There on the bottom shelf among six of this and six of that was a single glass — the one missing from Ackroyd's office.

Palmer called for Iris. She was still tearful and looked pale. I reckoned it would not take much to push her over her limit and cause her to faint. The female constable followed her closely and I guessed she was as worried about the state of health of Iris as I was.

'Where did you get this glass?' Palmer asked.

'John must have picked it up somewhere and changed his mind about keeping it,' she said. 'I found it in the kitchen bin. Seemed too good to throw away. Handy for a glass of sherry, if anyone asked for one.'

Or Madeira.

Palmer told the SOCO to bag it and we left in high spirits — or just the saving grace of sherry. We drove back with flashing lights and siren going, impatient to drag Samson back into the interview room. We'd got him at last.

Samson and Harrison, his lawyer, entered the room. I could tell by the slump in his shoulders that Samson knew from our expressions, to quote a well-worn phrase, that the game was up. Time for 'I dunnit, it's a fair cop.'

'Tell us about the glass,' Palmer said.

'What glass?' said Samson.

'The one in your dresser.'

Samson's face lost all colour.

'Why,' Palmer asked, 'didn't you just throw it out of your car window on the way home or dump it in a bin by a bus stop? Or some other place where it wouldn't be found, rather than putting it in your bin when you got home. Your wife is a frugal woman. She rescued it from landfill.'

'My client has no comment,' Harrison said.

'Follow the money trail,' I said. 'We've talked to your bank. That leads to you and Jenkins being fifty-fifty shareholders.'

'No comment.'

'Why did Ackroyd have to die?' I asked. 'Just to stop us carrying out the valuation and not have any chance of uncovering your planned fraud? And why the heavies? Another go at persuasion?'

Palmer had lost patience. 'John Samson. I am charging you with the murder of Roger Ackroyd. You do not—' I tuned out; I knew the rest.

A uniformed officer took him away for a night in the cells and the hope of cutting a deal, admitting everything and getting a lighter sentence. No chance.

Back to Jenkins. Harrison hard on her heels.

'I have arrested Samson for the murder of Roger Ackroyd. I think it's time we looked again at what you told us before. Samson was a fool. He kept the glass, or rather, his wife did. He will spend the rest of his life in prison. What about you? Do you still want to cut that deal?'

She looked at Harrison and he nodded. 'Recommendation to the judge for a lighter sentence because of cooperation and a statement of guilt?' he said.

'I'll do what I can,' said Palmer, which I guessed was nothing. 'Now, talk.'

'It was John's idea,' she said. 'We'd started having an affair about two months ago. He was bored with his wife and his life in general, too — having no money, no treats, no sex as well. His dream was dumping the wife and kids, buying a house in Barbados and retiring in luxury. With me by his side, naturally, sitting on loungers by the pool sipping rum punches. We were having dinner at some swanky restaurant he'd picked, pretending I was a client and he was entertaining me.' She paused. 'Look,' she said. 'I need a cigarette. Take me outside for a minute, and then I'll carry on with the full story.'

Palmer looked at the uniformed officer guarding the door and asked to borrow his handcuffs. He put them on Jenkins and led her to the front of the building, Harrison following. Palmer took her cigarettes and an expensive gold-plated lighter — a present from Samson, I assumed, another entry in the maxed credit card statement — from the black bag that held her possessions and we all went outside. She lit it up, blew a cloud into the air and sighed with pleasure.

'That's what you get when you cooperate,' Palmer said.

'Bear that in mind when the case comes up,' Harrison said.

She dragged on the cigarette down to the filter, dropped it on the ground and stubbed it out with her shoe. She took another from the pack and lit it.

'Might as well get my money's worth,' she said. 'It could be the last opportunity I get for a while.'

Canning came out of the building as we were standing there. I walked over to him to say goodbye. 'I've printed everything out,' he said. 'They planned it well. Why choose an account in Britain, though? You need an anonymous bank offshore somewhere for that kind of money. They were aiming to get five million. Nice round number. Would have set them up for life. What put you on to it?'

'They did a trial run. Someone complained at the lateness of receiving the money. Plus the fact that the practice had no money. The client account had all the big money. It was always vulnerable for a crooked accounts manager and one of the solicitors, let alone three.'

Then there were lots of small things, too, I thought. The double life of Jenkins — the butterfly emerging from the husk of the cocoon. Samson's obvious unhappiness with his life, stowing away the wedding photo out of sight. Taking everything together, a tie-in between Jenkins and some man from Ackroyds was always the likely pair to raid the conveyancing money. I didn't know for certain that it was Samson until they tried to do a runner — too many fingers in the conveyancing pie to be sure. Baker and Seymour were an added bonus.

'Good to see you again,' Canning said. 'You must come for dinner one night.'

'I would like that,' I said. 'It would be good to see your family again. Thanks, again.'

We shook hands and he walked to the tube station to get to Liverpool Street and the train to his new home in Colchester.

Jenkins finished her second cigarette and Palmer ushered her inside before she lit a third. We walked back to the interview room where Palmer took off the handcuffs and returned them to the uniformed officer guarding the door. We took our places for the continuation of her confession.

'He said it in a jokey manner,' she said, 'saying how easy it would be to divert money from the client account. What would I do with five million pounds?

'We decided on the last Friday in the month, when the transactions became hectic. We settled on two hours of diverting and did the trial. That showed us that no one was going to create a fuss before even longer. We extended our target time to three hours to ensure we had enough money to fulfil our dreams. Divert the money, get the suitcases from our cars and off to Heathrow. Couldn't be easier. That was his plan. I worked out the addition of Baker and Seymour. The double-cross of all three of them.'

'And then we came along,' I said, 'with our forensic examination of the practice's finance? You could have postponed the sting. Why didn't you do that?'

'There was the problem of the takeover by Randall. Would I have the job after that? It was now or never. It had to go ahead.'

'And then things got messy,' Palmer said. 'The whole scheme would fall apart if Shannon had come across the trial run and worked out the importance of it. What next?'

'Our only hope, at that stage, was to get the contract cancelled from our side,' she said.

'Which meant Ackroyd had to die?' Palmer said.

'It wasn't something we thought of lightly,' she said.

'Glad about that,' Palmer said, deadpan.

'Don't joke, inspector. I'd expect that from Shannon, not you. The plans were made. Too late to go back.'

'And the murder?' I asked. 'Whose idea was it to poison him?'

'John's. He said that, at his age, Ackroyd wouldn't notice the strychnine because of the Madeira. He said that when you're young, your tastebuds haven't developed, and you start with sweet drinks. When you grow older your tastebuds are more sensitive, and you move on to drinks that are dry to the taste. When old, your tastebuds decline and you move back to sweet drinks.'

'Like Madeira?' I said.

'Exactly,' she said. 'He googled around and saw how easy it was to make strychnine from weedkiller. From then on, the die was cast. There was no going back.'

'How did you get the heavies? The two men with the jackhammer?'

'John had got them off an assault and battery charge when the odds were stacked against them and the expectation was that they would do a spell in jail. John won the case; some technicality. They were eternally grateful. It was easy to call in favours. Shame it didn't work. Couldn't even get you under the wheels of a taxi. All we needed was time.'

'The plan was?' said Palmer.

'I would set off the alarm — we needed the disruption it would cause. John would have come through the French doors and be having the drink and cake with Ackroyd, and he would slip the strychnine in his drink. John knew how to set up a trick with the French doors — he'd seen it in some TV drama. What did it matter?' she said. 'Ackroyd was old. Where was the prickle in our consciences?'

'I know a few million older people who wouldn't agree with you,' said Palmer.

'But fraud is a crime where normal standards don't apply,' I said. 'It's driven by greed, and greed knows no boundaries. Conscience is the first thing to go.'

'Any chance of bail?' Harrison asked.

Palmer nearly choked on a coughing fit. 'You must be joking,' he managed to say. 'Fraud? Murder? What do you think?'

'Just thought I'd ask,' said Harrison. 'No harm in asking.'

'Take her away,' Palmer said to the constable.

Harrison followed Jenkins from the room. That would be the last time I saw her.

Palmer turned to me. 'I don't do this very often, Shannon, so make the most of it.' He extended his hand to me. 'Thanks,' he said.

CHAPTER FORTY-TWO

There was only one place for the celebration. We assembled at Toddy's, fine food and friendly atmosphere. Cherry and Anji were wearing little black dresses and looked radiant: it was good to see Anji choose a dress that she had worn to bait Randall. It signalled she was over that episode. Morag had on a skirt suit of grey with a tailored jacket and a plain gold necklace. Arthur was in his customary donkey jacket — when you found something that fits, why not keep wearing it? Norman had a blazer with gold buttons and a crisp white shirt that Morag had ironed for him earlier. I was wearing some black chinos and a matching long-sleeve shirt. And then there was our newest recruit, in a beige suit and dark brown shirt. Beryl.

'This is a real treat,' she said. 'I haven't eaten out for such a long time now. I managed to get a neighbour to sit with my husband and look after him and the cats for a few hours. Freedom for a while. I intend to make the most of it.'

'And how was Ackroyds after I left?' I asked.

'Gloomy,' she said. 'Randall lost no time in issuing the redundancy letters. The staff have been cut to the bone. There's hardly anyone left from the support staff. All that loyalty gone in a few hours.'

'If it's any consolation, we fixed Randall on two fronts — our invoice, ungratefully paid, and his blatant sexism. When we left, he was not a happy bunny. We hit him in his wallet and his pants. Big time.'

'Our redundancy payments were sorted,' Beryl said. 'Fiona came to see us all personally and handed out cheques. We all got six months' pay. More than anyone had dreamed of. That sugared the pill, but it's sad to be losing all those friends.'

'Take your time,' Norman said, in extra special jubilant mood. 'When you're ready there's a job here for you. This has been our most lucrative job ever, and you played a role in that success.'

'And in getting our own back on Jinx,' added Anji. 'For that I'm grateful.'

'It was fun,' Beryl said. 'What exciting lives you lead. I'd so like to be one of your team. When the time is right, that is.'

'Let's not talk of sad things,' Cherry said. 'Tonight is for celebration. You should have seen Randall's face when we handed him our invoice.' She laughed. 'Frozen into alabaster. As Norman said, this has been our most lucrative job. We'd like you all to have a bonus. Five thousand for each of you: Anji for her persevering with Randall in what must have been a distasteful business; Morag for her shopping in Tottenham Court Road and the antiques shops, and Arthur for his late-night stints in his van. Which brings me to you, Beryl: we'd like you to have a thousand pounds. Go hit the shops with Anji and splash the cash.'

'Good speech, Walker,' I said.

'Thanks, Shannon,' she replied, with a smile.

'Shame that Ackroyd had to die,' Beryl said, 'even though he wasn't as saintly as I thought. He was a kind man, and I will miss his afternoon Madeira breaks. Not many of his age left anymore.'

'We have to take some responsibility for that,' said Norman. 'It would be good to have some permanent reminder of him. A bench in the Temple garden, maybe?'

'That would be perfect,' Beryl said. 'He always liked looking out over the garden.

'I'll organize it,' said Morag. 'I doubt it would cost much . . .'

'And we have a lot of money sloshing around,' I finished.

'It will be a fitting gesture,' Morag continued.

'Let's order,' said Arthur. 'I'm starving. And another bottle of fizz wouldn't go amiss.'

The waiter came over. 'Toddy said he will do you a platter to share for your first course. What would you like for your mains? He's managed to get hold of a suckling pig which he roasts with home-made apple and quince sauce. I can highly recommend it.'

We looked at each other. Norman said, 'Why not?'

Decision made. One of the easiest we had had to make over the last couple of weeks. A sharing platter among friends. How appropriate.

And that's how the whole sorry mess ended. Except it wasn't all sorrow.

CHAPTER FORTY-THREE

It was ten a.m. on the Saturday morning and I was sitting in the downstairs room overlooking the river, nursing a hangover. I was debating the wisdom of making a third cup of coffee when Anji walked in. 'And how is Ms Winterbottom this morning?' I asked.

She scowled at me.

'It's Anji,' she said.

I smiled. 'Just Anji.'

THE END

ALSO BY PAUL BENNETT

NICK SHANNON THRILLERS
Book 1: DUE DILIGENCE
Book 2: COLLATERAL DAMAGE
Book 3: FALSE PROFITS
Book 4: THE MONEY RACE
Book 5: BLUE ON BLUE
Book 6: SHANNON'S LAW

JOHNNY SILVER THRILLERS
Book 1: MERCENARY
Book 2: KILLER IN BLACK
Book 3: ONE BULLET TOO MANY
Book 4: NO EASY WAY OUT

STANDALONE NOVELS
CATALYST

Thank you for reading this book.

If you enjoyed it please leave feedback on Amazon or Goodreads, and if there is anything we missed or you have a question about, then please get in touch. We appreciate you choosing our book.

Founded in 2014 in Shoreditch, London, we at Joffe Books pride ourselves on our history of innovative publishing. We were thrilled to be shortlisted for Independent Publisher of the Year at the British Book Awards.

www.joffebooks.com

We're very grateful to eagle-eyed readers who take the time to contact us. Please send any errors you find to corrections@joffebooks.com. We'll get them fixed ASAP.